Witch
and Tell

Angela M. Sanders

Kensington Publishing Corp.
kensingtonbooks.com

KENSINGTON BOOKS are published by

Kensington Publishing Corp.
900 Third Avenue
New York, NY 10022

All Kensington titles, imprints, and distributed lines are available at special quantity discounts for bulk purchases for sales promotion, premiums, fund-raising, educational, or institutional use.

Special book excerpts or customized printings can also be created to fit specific needs. For details, write or phone the office of the Kensington Sales Manager: Attn.: Sales Department. Kensington Publishing Corp., 900 Third Avenue, New York, NY 10022. Phone: 1-800-221-2647.

KENSINGTON and the KENSINGTON COZIES teapot logo Reg US Pat. & TM Off.

First Printing: November 2025
ISBN: 978-1-4967-5644-2

ISBN: 978-1-4967-5645-9 (ebook)

10 9 8 7 6 5 4 3 2 1

Printed in the United States of America

The authorized representative in the EU for product safety and compliance is eucomply OU, Parnu mnt 139b-14, Apt 123
Tallinn, Berlin 11317, hello@eucompliancepartner.com

THE BODY IN THE LIBRARY

I forced myself to open the door of my apartment and peer over the railing to the atrium. The moon was new, and I couldn't make out much from the scant light shining through the roof's stained-glass cupola. The portrait of Marilyn Wilfred over the front entrance was cloaked in darkness. Something black and sizable lay in the atrium—I thought it did, anyway.

"Hello?" I said, my voice wavering. "Is anybody there?"

I heard nothing but the relentless cawing of the crows. The books remained silent. Despite the summer night's heat, my skin prickled. I swallowed and turned for the service stairwell.

At ground level, the lump became clearer. It was a person, inert, lying on his side.

"Hello?" I ventured again. Nothing. Even the crows had stopped their shrieks.

I crept closer. A man, dressed in black, faced away from me. Did someone break in and fall, drunk perhaps, on the floor? Gingerly, I edged around the form, keeping my distance in case he should leap up.

Now that I saw him, it was clear there would be no leaping up—not now, not ever. . . .

Books by Angela M. Sanders

BAIT AND WITCH

SEVEN-YEAR WITCH

WITCH AND FAMOUS

WITCH UPON A STAR

GONE WITH THE WITCH

THE WITCH IS BACK

WITCH AND TELL

Published by Kensington Publishing Corp.

To JD, Rich, and Kirby

Chapter One

Lalena's text was urgent: I need to see you. Can you meet me at my place?

I wasted no time setting aside *The Body in the Library*, the Agatha Christie mystery I was rereading, and locking my apartment in the old servant's quarters in the Victorian mansion that served as Wilfred's library.

My cat Rodney trotted ahead of me as I hurried down the hill on foot. It was a warm day, the kind of August afternoon in which Oregon excelled. The breeze through the woods smelled of pine needles, and the sky was rich blue and streaked with clouds, like the Florentine endpaper in leather-bound novels.

Rodney's sleek black form darted through the tidy double row of trailers that made up the Magnolia Rolling Estates and passed under the rosebushes surrounding LALENA'S PALM READINGS HERE sign. I rapped on her screen door and opened it to find her at her kitchen table, her head flat on its linoleum surface, tarot cards splayed around her.

"Lalena? I got here as soon as I could."

Rodney dashed through the door to greet Lalena's terrier mutt, Sailor. He jumped to the couch and batted Sailor's head before settling next to him.

"Josie." Lalena raised her head. The colorful scarf she'd wound around her head and her vivid lipstick didn't distract me from her unwashed hair and tired eyes. "Thank you for coming. Help yourself to iced tea."

I poured each of us a glass from her refrigerator and joined her at the table. "What's wrong?"

"It's about Ian. I don't know what to do."

Ian Penclosa was Lalena's boyfriend. They'd met less than a year ago when he moved to town to open a rare books stall in Patty's This-N-That. They were an unusual couple—Lalena, bubbly and open; Ian, shy and intense—but it had been love at first sight. On walks through town, Lalena kept a hand on Ian's shoulder while he maneuvered his wheelchair through the streets.

"What happened to him?" I asked.

"We haven't talked for two days."

I leaned back in relief. "That's all? You had me worried."

She raised her head and leveled a sour look at me. "Two days is an eternity. We're soulmates, Josie." She collapsed on the table again but held up a tarot card. "This morning I drew this. The Ten of Swords."

I took the card from her fingers. It featured a man flat on his belly, stabbed through his back with an armload of swords. It was hard to put a positive spin on this one. "Maybe he's getting acupuncture?"

"It means death. Termination. Something bad has happened." She snatched the card from my fingers and threw it on the floor, where it skittled to a stop under the refrigerator.

I tried again. "It's still a new relationship. Maybe he's having a little freak-out. Maybe he just needs to back off for a while before moving forward."

"That's not it," she said. "Just last week we were talking about what it would be like to grow old together." Her gaze took a faraway look. "We were going to take a cruise on the Bosphorus. Ian had been studying the pagan religions of Turkey."

This would be par for the course for Ian, as a dealer in books on parapsychology and the occult. For his birthday breakfast, Lalena had fried hash browns shaped like pentacles.

"Maybe all you need is a good talk. Clear the air," I said.

"Look how well that worked for you."

Ouch. Lalena was right, although she'd never know the details. Since I'd told Sam, Wilfred's sheriff and my boyfriend, that I was a witch, our communication had collapsed. I was heartbroken.

She reached across the table and touched my hand. "I'm sorry. That was low. Have you heard from Sam lately? I know he's been out of town."

I looked at the tabletop and shook my head. Sam was in D.C. on an art theft case, but he had a phone and computer. Still no response to my texts and calls. "We're not here to talk about me."

She straightened and rubbed her throat as if a lump were forming there. "It's worse than I've made out. Ian. . . ."

I nodded. "Yes?"

"Ian won't talk to me at all. I reach out, nothing." Anguish crept into her voice. "I don't know what's wrong. I don't know if it's me, or if something's happened to him." She pulled her phone from the counter behind her and tapped its screen. "He left me this message the day before yesterday."

Ian's voice came from the tiny speaker. "Lalena . . . listen, I've got to go. I'll be in touch. Take care."

"That's it." She set the phone face down on the table. "I don't know what to make of it. It's not so much that he had to go somewhere, but that he wouldn't tell me about it."

How I felt her pain. "Let's start at the beginning. When did he start to shut down? Or did it happen all at once?"

She drew a long breath. "Three days ago. I've thought about it over and over. We were at Darla's Café, and he was in the middle of relating some old doctor's theory of garden fairies when he went blank." Lalena's expression froze as she mimicked Ian's face. "Mid-sentence. It was so weird, as if he'd seen a ghost." She contemplated this a moment. "Bad comparison, since he'd be psyched to see a ghost. Anyway, you know what I mean. We finished dinner, but something had changed."

"That doesn't sound like him."

"It gets worse," she said. "We had a date the next day

to hit up some estate sales for books. He never showed. Then I got this message." She lifted her phone. "I had a client, so I couldn't pick up. Raylene Burns, you know, from the feed store. She has a new beau and needed a psychic consultation."

I nodded. Raylene's romantic exploits were conversational fodder around town. Word was, she had her eye on the horse supplements salesman. "Was it something Ian was talking about? Or saw at the café?"

She lifted Sailor to her lap. "I don't think so. There was nothing around us but diners. The regulars, plus a few construction workers from the renovation at the Empress." Her shoulders fell. "Oh, Josie. I don't know what to do. I'm worried. What if something happened to him?"

Our tumblers of iced tea had turned lukewarm, and condensation puddled on the tabletop. I turned the glass in my hand and nodded across the trailer park. "His van is still in his driveway, so he couldn't have gone far. Maybe he took a cab to the airport for an emergency trip home. Lots of cab companies have vans that accommodate wheelchairs. Have you been in touch with his family?"

"I haven't met them."

"We could track them down. Where's Ian from?"

She hesitated a moment before saying, "I don't know. The East Coast somewhere."

That much I'd gathered from his accent. Although my research skills were good, they weren't good enough to query the entire eastern seaboard. Lalena's mournful expression led me to add, "I wish there was something I could do for you."

She pushed her tarot cards into a pile. "There is something you could do. You could look for him. Would you do that?" She bit her lip. "I'm . . . I'm embarrassed to ask myself, and I'm worried."

And hurt. I got that. "Sure. I'll ask if anyone's seen him lately. I bet it's all a simple misunderstanding."

"I'd appreciate it so much. Thank you." She gathered the tarot cards. "Mostly, I want to know he's okay. But, if he is, could you find out why he's been out of touch?"

This part I was less comfortable with. "What if it's personal? It should be you who talks to him."

The hurt in her eyes was palpable. "And say what?"

I understood. I relented. "All right. But I'm not digging too deeply. If he doesn't want to talk, I'm not pushing it."

"You're a good friend, Josie." She set Sailor on the floor and came to my side of the table. "Stand up. I want to give you a hug."

Crushed in Lalena's arms, I glanced at the couch, where Rodney stared with unblinking amber eyes, seeming to say, *Good luck with this one.*

Chapter Two

As I left Lalena's, I decided that now was as good a time as any to buttonhole Ian. It was Sunday, my day off, and other than a trip to the P.O. Grocery to stock my refrigerator, the day was open.

I hadn't said anything to Lalena, but I wondered how well she really knew Ian. He wouldn't talk about his life before coming to Wilfred, and I wasn't the only person who'd noticed his trick of changing the conversation when it ventured into his past.

I understood Lalena's draw to him. When he smiled, his demeanor became almost childlike. His eyes warmed from onyx black to tiger's-eye brown, and friendly lines appeared. His laughter was goofy, and he ordered glasses of milk at the tavern. Orson, the bartender, kept a gallon of two percent at the ready for him.

I hadn't always felt that way about Ian. His usual expression was impassive, unreadable. My magic came from books—they talked to me—and although most of the books Ian sold sang Gregorian chants and lectured on divination, a few had hissed and crackled in a way that sent prickles down my arms.

That is, if the books spoke at all. Something had been interfering with my magic lately. Instead of the books' clear voices, their messages often came through with static. Sometimes I couldn't even make them out. It worried me.

One thing I could do now, though, was to help La-lena. Chances were good that if Ian was in town, he'd be at the This-N-That antiques mall. Most of the other dealers stocked their booths after hours, but Ian kept a corner of his area free for a small desk where he filled internet orders and chatted with customers.

The bell at the This-N-That's door chimed as I opened it. The ceiling fan rippled my hair.

"Welcome, Josie," Thor said from his seat on the counter. He threw back the edge of the cape he habitually wore, even to elementary school.

"Where's your eyepatch?" I asked. Despite having two working eyes, Thor wore his eyepatch everywhere.

"Buffy broke the elastic, and Grandma won't buy me a new one."

Thor's younger sister Buffy popped from the other side of the counter, holding a collapsible fan in one hand and rubber bands in the other. "I'm making him another one." A calculating look crossed her face. "It's a warm day. Perhaps you'd like me to follow you around the store and fan you?"

"For a modest fee, of course," I said. These kids were constantly on the prowl for money.

"Naturally. You would want to pay a poor little girl

for her work, wouldn't you?" Buffy actually batted her eyes.

"No, thank you. I'm fine. Is Ian in?"

Realizing she couldn't turn a buck with me, Buffy retreated behind the counter. Thor picked up his comic book. "Nope."

Ian's stall was directly to the left of the cashier's counter. I was relieved to feel the books' energy as they murmured hellos only I could hear. I brushed fingers over a row of leather-bound spines with gold embossed titles and felt a tingle of magic rush through my palms as the books gasped and sighed. A treatise on alchemy lectured with a German-inflected accent.

"Books," I whispered, "where is Ian?"

Gone, disparû, verschwunden, vanished, the books replied.

The books' message wasn't reassuring, but it was so good to hear their voices. Besides the drop in my ability to siphon magical energy from books, other strange things had been happening. Candles snuffed out by themselves. Mirrors refused to return my reflection for the span of a few blinks. Flowers deadened in their vases overnight, and I periodically smelled wafts of sulfur. And the crows—rivers of crows. They crowded the branches of the oak outside my bedroom window and cawed, even at night when they should be roosting.

Something—or someone—was stealing my magic, and I was unsure how to prevent it.

Rodney twisted around my ankles and rose to stand on his back legs so I could scratch his chin. He was an honored citizen in Wilfred and let in just about everywhere except the café, which, because of county health regulations, banned animals. That didn't stop him from sneaking in from time to time to cadge a forkful of salmon.

"Josie, I was hoping I'd run into you. I just got back from an estate sale and have a few things that might interest you."

Babe Hamilton stood outside Ian's stall, holding a box. Her stall was stocked with vintage textiles. I'd already bought enough linen napkins to host dinner parties for twelve. A stranger could see Babe's style in her chic eyeglasses and simple but well-cut dresses on her comfortable frame. I knew her taste from the amazing fabrics and old French *torchon*s she somehow harvested within a few hours' drive of Wilfred.

"Let me take that box," I said. Babe was hardly elderly—I pegged her as in her sixties, a bit older than my mother—but linens were heavy. Besides, I wanted to get first dibs on whatever the box held.

"Thank you." Babe led the way to her lavender-scented shelves. "You can set it on the floor."

I rested the box next to a table holding chenille bedspreads. "Have you seen Ian lately?"

She wrinkled her brow. "No, come to think of it. Not here or at home." Babe lived in the mobile home behind Lalena's at the Magnolia Rolling Estates. "Not for a few days."

The This-N-That's doorbell chimed again, and Buffy and Thor's voices greeted the newcomer. "Hi, Wanda. Will you require our help?" Buffy asked. "We offer guided tours at a reasonable price."

Where did Buffy get her patter? She sounded like a shopping network host, not a seven-year-old girl.

"No thanks, you little shysters. I can find my way around just fine."

I didn't know Wanda well, just that she was the new custodian at the retreat center and Duke's sister. Duke, Wilfred's jack-of-all-trades extraordinaire, was a town fixture, and all it had taken was his recommendation to secure his sister a job.

My upbeat mood faded when I saw Wanda's face. She stepped back, as if startled. She smiled, but it was the kind of smile someone affects when the dentist asks if everything's okay. She pointed at my feet. "I see you have a cat."

"That's Rodney," I said. I looked down. Rodney had vanished. "At least, he was here a second ago." Something in her tone of voice led me to add, "He's friendly."

Wanda's smile labored on. "Is that so?"

"Have you by chance seen Ian Penclosa up by the retreat center?"

Wanda shook her head and ran a finger through scruffy, steel gray hair. "We have a short-term visitor, a young lady, who came a few days ago. That's it. But about the cat. Does it run free?" Her voice was remarkably clear and loud. Had she not gone into janitorial work, she might have had a career on the stage.

"Yes," I said. What was she getting at? Babe shrugged and ducked back into her stall. "But like I said, he's perfectly friendly."

She made a sound I couldn't quite read and backed

for the door. Then she was gone. Whatever she'd come to the This-N-That for apparently could wait.

Very strange. Maybe she was allergic. I retreated to Ian's stall to let the books soothe me with their murmurs of runes, ancient texts, and crystal balls. Rodney reappeared and leapt to Ian's corner desk. He purred as I stroked his back and ran a finger up his tail. "I think Wanda's afraid of you, little guy."

Rodney flicked his tail, knocking one of Ian's business cards from its holder, a plastic skull, to the floor. I picked it up. Ian. Where could he be?

"Buffy, Thor," I said.

"Yes?" Thor slipped down from the counter and trotted around the corner to Ian's stall. He now wore Buffy's homemade eyepatch, which featured a heavily lashed eyeball crayoned on it.

"Would you like to earn some money?"

Buffy joined her brother. "How much?"

"Five big ones. Each," I said.

Thor nodded vigorously, but Buffy replied, "Ten."

"Seven fifty."

Thor and Buffy looked at each other. Buffy said, "Okay. What do we have to do?"

"Find Ian and let me know where he is. I'll be at the café for dinner at six, ready for your report." Neither of the kids budged. "What are you waiting for?" Their grandmother Patty ran the cash register. It wasn't as if they were needed.

"Cash, please," Buffy said.

I took a five-dollar bill and change from my purse. "Part now, the rest later."

"Ten-four," Thor said, and made for the door.

Chapter Three

Summer nights in Wilfred were worth waiting for all year. The day's heat settled into a soft warmth that encouraged thrown-open windows, and crickets chirped in the meadow. Sundays were especially nice. The aromas of roast beef and fresh pie drifted through screen doors, and kids played outside until porch lights switched on and mothers called them in.

Until lately, my Sunday evenings had been spent at Sam's. I'd looked forward to them all week. Sam was a wonderful cook, and I was turning into a decent prep chef. We'd take our plates to the small porch off the kitchen and watch the lights in Wilfred, below the river, twinkle on as the sun set. A baby gate across the steps was enough to keep his toddler son Nicky playing at our feet but was no barrier to Rodney, who leapt over it and plopped nearby, flicking his tail.

That was then. Tonight I was at Darla's Café, awaiting the fried chicken special. Alone. The patio was no substitute for Sam's kitchen porch, and the neighbors surrounding me—friendly as they were—were no substitute for Sam. Wherever he was. I looked at my phone. Five texts I'd sent him over the past few days, and he hadn't responded to a single one. Was he still in D.C., testifying on the stolen art case? Or was he simply avoiding me now that I'd confessed I was a witch?

My heart ached. I returned my phone to my pocket.

Darla clearly read the sadness on my face. Wilfred was small enough that no one's business remained private for long, and she knew something was up between Sam and me. "Here you go, honey," she said, and slid a platter of chicken and potato salad next to my tumbler of iced tea. "I'll bring you a slice of Marionberry pie. On the house."

I managed a weak smile in return. No Sam, and my magic was on the rocks, too. As my mood cratered, voices at the patio's edge caught my attention.

"Work starts early tomorrow, Cliff," a man said. The lenses of his sunglasses glinted in the fading sunlight. He slipped them off to reveal surprisingly warm eyes. Darla had pointed him out a few days earlier. He was in charge of the construction crew turning the Empress Theater into a brewpub. "You can't be out partying all night."

The man's chiding tone caused his tablemate, Cliff, to face him head on. Like everyone else on the patio, I stopped eating to listen. I vaguely recognized Cliff from seeing him alight from a dented white van a morning earlier in the week. I'd glimpsed empty beer cans and a rumpled sleeping bag through the door behind him.

The renovations at the Empress, a long-abandoned

movie house from when Wilfred was a thriving timber town, had brought in a number of construction workers. Most drove in from nearby Gaston and Forest Grove, but a few camped out locally in vans or RVs.

"I'll do whatever I want." Cliff's tone was chilling. Who was the boss here, anyway?

The man with the sunglasses, now set beside his plate, tipped his head in warning. "I'll see you tomorrow, on time and ready to work."

Cliff's gaze skimmed the diners. He opened his mouth as if to speak, but seemed to think better of it. "All right." He left the patio and entered the café, likely to pass through to the tavern.

Orson appeared at my side before I could tuck my fork into my potato salad. Besides being the tavern's bartender, he owned the Empress. "A partier, that one," he said.

"You'd know, with your job," I said. "He hasn't made trouble, has he?"

"Not to speak of." Orson gazed thoughtfully at the café door through which Cliff had just disappeared. "He's more bark than bite. The man he was talking to? Construction manager. Drinks vodka martinis. Although. . . ."

Although, what? When it became clear that Orson wouldn't elaborate, I said, "Hey, who's watching the tavern?"

"Cutting back my hours. Ned Tohler has been at me for months for a spot behind the bar, so I'm finally giving it to him." Orson pulled out a chair and sat without asking. I didn't mind. It made me feel less alone. "You can expect tonier cocktails from now on."

The Tohler brood was sizable. Ned favored 1970s button-downs with wide lapels. I had no idea where he found his bell-bottom pants or white patent leather loafers, but I appreciated his style and predicted a profusion of Harvey Wallbangers and tequila sunrises to come. If I recalled correctly, his twin Ted ran a deli in nearby Gaston.

"Nope," Orson added. "Don't need to work now that the Empress is on its way to becoming a brewpub."

"Are you going to keep your place upstairs?" Orson had inherited the Empress from his father. For years the theater had sat with its windows boarded up and marquee dismantled. I'd thought the building was just another unused storefront until I'd had occasion to visit Orson. He'd converted the theater's projector room into a makeshift apartment with a mini-fridge and well-worn recliner.

"Yep. Finally getting windows. A proper kitchen, too. It's nice to see the old girl come back to life." He leaned back, crossing his ankles. "Soon we'll have lots of people here. Wilfred will be a destination, just like in the old days."

"Not just for a construction crew, either," I said, eyeing a few people who'd waved at the construction boss before settling at tables at the patio's edge. The renovation was giving Darla's business a definite boost. "It's hard to imagine town before the mill closed."

I'd seen photos in the library. The café had been a thriving soda counter, and the highway   a slender ribbon of road barely worthy of the name—was lined with businesses. Old cars, then new, parked at angles in front of the post office, a grocery store, a barber shop, and, of course, the Empress.

"It was a different town in those days," Orson said. "I still get a start when I go into the old post office and find it full of groceries."

The arrival of Buffy and Thor cut our conversation short. They ran to my table and rested their hands on the table's edge while they caught their breath. Thor drained my glass of water. Buffy reached for my iced tea, but I slid the glass toward me before she could take it.

"My cue to leave," Orson said. He'd been burned more than once by Buffy and Thor's moneymaking schemes. It had taken him two days to remove the furniture polish they'd used to wax his car. Orson tossed me a salute and crossed the patio, toward home.

Thor set down my empty glass and wiped his mouth. "It's a mystery."

"What's a mystery?" I said.

"Ian," Buffy said. "He's disappeared."

"Are you sure?" I asked. "You couldn't find him anywhere? Maybe he's away buying books for his stall." It broke my heart that Lalena could be right, and Ian had left town, leaving only a vague voicemail as a good-bye.

While I spoke, Thor was shaking his head. "Ian is totally gone. He's vanquished."

"Vanished," I corrected. "Are you sure?"

"Yes," Buffy said. "We did a complete investigation."

Thor took the chair Orson had vacated and flipped

his cape over its back. "First we checked the usual places."

"Grandma's"—Buffy referred to the This-N-That—"his trailer, and Aunt Darla's. He wasn't there."

"But his van is still in his driveway," I pointed out.

"I know," Thor said, clearly proud of his deduction. "No one saw a friend pick him up."

"Next step," Buffy said, "we got Duke's stepladder out of the shed and looked in Ian's windows."

"*I* looked in the windows." Thor tapped his chest. "Not you. You're too little to get on a ladder."

"I am not. Besides, I'm a lot more graceful than you. Grandma says."

"What did you see?" I asked. If they started bickering, I'd never get answers.

"Nothing." He folded his arms over his chest and leaned back. "But get this."

"Yes?"

"His milk was on the counter," Buffy said quickly.

Thor nudged his sister's shoulder. "I was going to tell her that!"

"A glass, or the whole carton?" I asked. Ian would never squander milk.

"Both," Thor said. "Pretty bad, huh?"

"So we checked places they might hide a body," Buffy said.

"You what?" I didn't want to speculate who *they* might be.

"That was my smart idea," Thor said. "Not Buffy's. We searched the stacking house, Lyndon's compost heap, and the dumpsters behind the Empress and the café."

"He might be in the millpond," Buffy added. Somehow she'd gotten hold of my iced tea after all and took a deep swig. "We looked around the edges but didn't see anything."

"Except Roz and Lyndon holding hands." Thor snickered.

"They're in love, dummy," Buffy said. She replaced my iced tea on the table and pulled a drumstick from my plate to crunch through its buttermilk crust.

"And the other lady, the one at the retreat center," Thor said.

The visitor Wanda had mentioned this afternoon at the This-N-That. Her arrival had roughly coincided with Ian's disappearance. I made a mental note to follow up. "What was she doing?"

Thor shrugged. "I don't know. Looking around, I guess."

"She didn't have a murder weapon, unless it was poison. Like, in a tiny jar." Buffy set the chicken bone, stripped clean, on my plate. "If you'd like us to continue looking, it will cost you. We take tips, too."

"That's enough for now," I told them. Their investigation had certainly taken a grisly turn. "Your tip is the half of my dinner you've eaten."

After they left, I picked up the remaining piece of chicken, now cold. For whatever reason, Ian had skipped town.

How much heartache could one tiny town hold? My pain alone was enough to cloud the valley. Add Lalena's sadness over Ian's disappearance, and together we could fill the millpond with tears.

"Here you go, honey." Darla deposited a slice of pie on my table, but my appetite was gone.

Chapter Four

"Everything will look better in the morning," goes the old saying, and in my case, it was true. The library was due to open in half an hour, and I made my rounds, basking in how lucky I was to work in such a magnificent place.

The library was housed in Thurston Wilfred's Italianate Victorian mansion. Thurston—known these days as Old Man Thurston—had left his home to his youngest daughter, Marilyn, who repurposed it into a library and left it to the town when she died almost thirty years ago.

Marilyn had converted the third-floor servants' quarters into an apartment, where I now lived. The rest of the mansion's rooms, including a conservatory, ranged around a central atrium topped with a stained-glass cupola. An open-air tower loomed above the mansion's front porch. Over the years, the library's Persian rugs had worn and leaded glass windows become wavy, but for me, it only added to the charm. Old Man Thurston's son built Big House across the garden, beyond the caretaker's cottage. As the last surviving Wilfred, Sam now lived there.

I started my rounds on the library's second floor, pulling open the faded brocade curtains in the old mansion's bedrooms, now full of books. Low morning sun flooded the rooms, washing the marble fireplaces with light and creating puddles of warmth on armchairs where Rodney had staked out a rotating selection of napping spots.

"Good morning, books," I said.

The books yawned and serenaded me with greetings. Birdsong escaped from a shelf in Natural History, and I heard a faraway disco beat and shouts to *feel the burn!* from Physical Fitness. My shoulders relaxed. The books talked to me this morning, and their voices were refreshingly loud and clear. Maybe the glitches in my magic had passed and were merely due to sunspots or some other energetic firestorm.

The only flaw I foresaw in my day was how I was going to tell Lalena I'd made zero progress finding Ian. That, and missing Sam, of course. Would I ever get used to it?

Downstairs, I started a pot of coffee in the kitchen. Most library regulars entered through the kitchen door, stopping for a chat and cup of coffee at the long wooden table. Some patrons never made it past the kitchen. I opened the casement window in my office off the kitchen—the mansion's former pantry under the main staircase—and let the breeze off the Kirby River fill the tiny space. I was happy not to see the crows that had been following me lately.

From there, I moved to the mansion's former drawing and dining rooms. Sun glinted off their chipped chandeliers. I opened the French doors in Circulation and couldn't help looking across the lawn. No sign of Sam.

Before opening for business, I stopped by the conservatory to say hello to Roz. Afternoons, she was assistant librarian, but mornings she kept for writing romance novels under her pen name, Eliza Chatterly Windsor. This one featured pirates.

"How's the new house coming?" I asked her. She and her husband Lyndon Forster, the library's caretaker, were building a home. Roz was happy to be getting a dedicated writing space, and Lyndon had already mapped out vegetable beds and a plumbed garden shed. I'd miss seeing her on weekday mornings.

"All right," Roz said, without lifting her fingers from her laptop's keyboard. I'd leave her be to her world of buccaneers—the romantic lead would likely be called Captain Forster Lyndon or another variation of her husband's name—and maidens, or dukes and orphaned spinsters, or whatever it was this time.

I unlocked the front door and settled at Circulation to greet the day's patrons, from the children's reading hour in Old Man Thurston's former office, to Mrs. Garlington's organ students in the late afternoon, to the knitting club members in the conservatory.

Before I could even start sorting returns, Lalena appeared through the open French doors. She glanced meaningfully toward Sam's empty driveway, then back to me. I looked away to hide my disappointment.

Her expression softened in sympathy. "No Sam yet?"

I shook my head. I'd have to get used to the idea that we weren't together anymore. "Any word from Ian?"

"No, but I did another tarot card reading this morning, and. . . ." She untied the ribbon that was Sailor's leash, and he trotted toward the atrium to search for Rodney. She dropped into a velvet upholstered chair and played with a loose thread on its arm.

"And what?"

"I pulled the Death card."

Oh, boy. I grabbed a stack of books from the returns cart to process. "I thought you didn't believe in tarot cards. You told me you use them as a tool for your customers to see whatever their subconscious has been storing up for them but that they don't want to recognize."

I didn't tell her about Buffy and Thor's search or about what they'd spied in his trailer. There was no use piling it on. For whatever reason, Ian wasn't in Wilfred. As for his van still parked outside his home, he might have called a cab. I had to hope there was an explanation that didn't have to do with his relationship with Lalena. Or, I thought, picturing the tarot card, something worse.

Lalena stabbed the air with a finger. "Exactly. Maybe my subconscious has been picking up subtle clues that Ian plans to leave me, and now that I see the Ten of Swords and the Death cards, I know what they mean. It's over between us."

"My subconscious has been telling me otherwise, because I'm not convinced," I said.

"I know." A long sigh escaped her. "I don't understand it. This is not like Ian. At all."

I turned away and busied myself logging book returns. "I'd better order more westerns for Duke. He runs through them like potato chips."

She sat straighter and squinted at me. "Josie?"

"Yes?"

"Look at me."

I resolutely kept my head down. "There sure were lots of books in the return bin today."

"Don't try to distract me. You know something, don't you?"

"Not really."

"Not really? That means you know at least part of something. What aren't you telling me?" She leaned forward. "Spill it, Josie."

I gained time by returning to my seat behind the circulation desk. Sooner or later, she'd learn the truth. "I asked Buffy and Thor to track down Ian."

Lalena nodded. "Great idea. If those two kids can't find him, no one can. And?"

"They think he's left town."

"But his van is in the driveway," Lalena said quickly.

"Thor says he left a carton of milk on his kitchen counter."

"Not just a glass? A whole carton?" she asked.

"That's what he says."

"That's serious. Maybe he wants me to think he's still here," she said. Her body seemed to collapse into itself. "But he's gone. He went somewhere. He didn't want to tell me."

"That's not necessarily true."

"The alternative is worse," she said. "He could be dead. Or in a hospital somewhere."

"Surely you don't think that. Have you called the hospitals?"

She stared at the chair's arm and nodded.

I gentled my voice. "Then you know better. Maybe you should file a missing person's report with the sheriff's office."

"He left me a voicemail message, remember?"

I couldn't argue with that. I opened my mouth to tell her there might be another reason for his disappearance—even though I had no idea of what it might be—but was interrupted by a voice at the entrance to Circulation.

"What is this?" Wanda, the retreat center's new custodian, held up a copy of *Puss in Boots*.

"Children's reading hour starts soon. That's this morning's book," I said. Mona, the volunteer who led the reading hour, fostered animals. Most of the books she chose featured animals, too. "Did someone leave it on the floor?" The children's section rapidly became an obstacle course if I didn't tend to it regularly.

Wanda flipped through its pages and raised an eyebrow. "It's about cats."

"Yes. *Puss in Boots* is a classic. Kids love it."

She stared at the book's cover. I remembered her hesitancy with Rodney. Cats must really freak her out.

"Do you know what this story is about?" she asked with a tight smile.

Puss in Boots tried to respond, but its words slowed and garbled, lowering in pitch like a record player running out of power. Alarm quickened my pulse. It was happening again. Something was interfering with my magic.

"Sure," I said. "It's about a cat who helps his master win the hand of a princess."

"Through lying. And murder."

"An evil ogre is killed, as I remember."

"Yes." She nodded slowly. "Yes. I see. It's a fairy tale."

"Right." What was her deal? "Can I help you find something?"

She seemed to snap out a reverie. "I'd like to volunteer here. Work at the retreat center is sporadic, and I want to put my skills to good use."

This was a surprise, but a welcome one. "Your timing is great. Dylan, our intern, is off to college soon, and we don't have a replacement. We'd love to have you. Could you come in, let's see"—I called up the calendar on my computer—"the day after tomorrow?"

She didn't even pause. "Definitely."

"Hi, Josie." Mona had arrived for the reading hour and had a box of crayons and stack of paper under one arm. Before long, the floor in Children's Literature would be covered with scrawled drawings of cats wearing boots.

"Mona, have you met Wanda? She's the new custodian at the retreat center. Wanda, Mona volunteers here, too. She runs the children's reading hour."

Wanda tapped *Puss in Boots*'s cover. "You chose this."

"Isn't it sweet?" Mona said.

"Mona loves animals," I added. "She fosters them."
I'd have to mention Wanda's phobia about cats to
Mona. Maybe Mona would even be able to bring her
around. One glance at a baby kitten suckling a bottle
would melt anyone's heart.

Wanda's response, if she'd intended any, was interrupted by Sailor racing into Circulation with Rodney at
his heels. Sailor jumped into Lalena's lap, and Rodney
froze a few feet from Wanda.

Her stiff smile unwavering, Wanda stepped toward
Rodney, who lowered to his haunches and backed
away. When he hit a chair, he spun and ran for the exit.
I heard the cat door flap a second later.

Wanda's smile momentarily faded, then lit up again,
tense and firm. "Good day, Josie. I'll see you soon."

Chapter Five

The afternoon was quiet. I waited for the books to resume their chatter, but they were mute. I slid a novel from a shelf in Popular Releases, willing it to communicate some of the Louisiana swamp and thunderstorms of its setting, but it was lifeless between my palms.

Sighing, I returned the book to its shelf. I was on my way to my office when I saw one of the construction workers from the Empress hesitating at the entrance to the atrium.

"Can I help you?" I asked.

"This is a library? I know the sign outside says it is, but I've never seen a library like this."

Now I recognized the man—he was the construction worker I'd seen arguing with his boss at Darla's Café. Why wasn't he at work?

"Yes, it's a library. Crazy, isn't it? Looking for something to read?" If I remembered right, he slept in his van. He probably wanted somewhere to hang out with proper upholstery. Or maybe he'd heard about our claw-foot bathtub.

"Do you have some kind of program for visitors?" he asked.

"We have cards for temporary residents. You're working on the Empress, right? Come in to Circulation, and I'll set you up."

Head craning to take in moldings, paintings, and books, he followed me to the mansion's former drawing room.

"Have a seat." I turned to the computer monitor. "What's your name?"

"Cliff Montgomery." He slid his driver's license across the desk.

I stopped typing. "Like the actor?" Dylan, our intern obsessed with Hollywood's golden age, would love this.

"Uh-huh."

Up close, Cliff had his namesake's craggy brows and sharp jaw, but that's where the resemblance ended. This Cliff was a dirty blond, and his eyes were small enough that they almost disappeared when he smiled. In contrast, his mouth was broad and expressive. He wore work clothes—bright orange T-shirt, canvas pants, boots—but they were clean, not caked with drywall dust as I'd have expected. Maybe he'd changed before he came up here.

"I have to apologize," he said.

"For what?"

"I saw you at the café. You overheard my discussion

with Tyrone." His shook his head. "That should have never happened."

For a moment I considered pretending I hadn't heard, but he was being honest, so I was, too. "Don't worry about it. We all have disagreements with our bosses from time to time. How are things going at the Empress?"

He scooted his chair forward. "It's just a personality thing. Nothing more. He's so flashy, and I'm more down-to-earth. Know what I mean?"

Again, I stopped typing and looked at him. He really wanted to set me straight. "I can see how you might be different people."

"Exactly," he said, clearly pleased I agreed. "I'm a simple man. He's not. We don't understand each other, that's all."

Why was he telling me this? "I see."

"If I can add a warning, he's a player. I'm only saying so because you remind me of my sister, Mindy. You're an attractive lady—"

"Thank you."

"—and I wouldn't be surprised if he tries to make time with you. Watch out." He leaned back in his chair and crossed his legs.

I could have told him I had a boyfriend, but I couldn't honestly say that anymore. Sam and I hadn't officially broken up, but what else is it when someone refuses to respond to your texts and calls? "Noted." I walked to the printer to pick up his temporary card and handed it to him. "Now, what would you like to read?"

"There's something else." He sat straight. "I'd be careful about believing what he says."

"What do you mean?"

"He has some odd ideas, that's all. Take whatever he says with a grain of salt. He's been involved in shady activities."

Curious. "What kinds of activities?"

He looked around, then leaned forward and lowered his voice. "Let's put it this way: he has a record."

I wasn't sure how to respond to that. "Have you worked with him long?"

My question seemed to fluster Cliff. Finally, he met my eyes. "Long enough." He tucked the card into his wallet. "Now, what do you recommend?"

Normally the books would have flooded my head with titles. I would have known if he favored thrillers, preferred history, or even had a secret yen for romance novels. But this morning, they were silent.

Cliff must have seen the disappointment on my face. "Did I say something wrong?"

"No," I said quickly. "Not at all. Tell me what you usually read."

"What do you have in the line of true crime?"

Compared with my strange episodes with Wanda and Cliff, the rest of the day had been uneventful. Mr. Loveheart had dropped another novel in the river, where he'd been fishing. The library's trustees had told me long ago to expect regular losses from his fishing expeditions, but that his annual gift to the book buying fund more than made up for it. Mrs. Garlington's student had not shown up for organ lessons, so Mrs. Garlington had treated the library's patrons to a few spritely renditions of songs from the musical *Cats*. Word had already made the rounds about my *Puss in Boots* discussion with Wanda.

The evening—another without Sam—loomed ahead of me. I planned to put it to use. There was still one avenue open to finding Ian, and that was the stranger at the retreat center. Maybe her arrival had somehow scared him off.

My excuse to visit was that the retreat center housed a satellite library for visitors. I filled a tote bag with thrillers, mysteries, romance, science fiction, and fantasy, and I was pleased to hear their curious blend of squealing tires, dragon's roars, and lovers' sighs. My magic was edging back after the afternoon's lull. Rodney wound around my ankles, letting his silky tail brush my calf. "You'd better stay here, baby. Just in case you scare Wanda."

I took the trail along the river to the retreat center. The sun was low enough that it filtered through the fir trees, but night wouldn't fall for hours yet. To my left stood forest, and to my right sloped the embankment to the cottonwood trees along the drowsy Kirby River. Beyond the river spread the few blocks of Wilfred proper.

I stood for a moment to take in the view. Cars filled the parking lot at Darla's, and the tidy rows of trailers at the Magnolia Rolling Estates lay at an angle like bones along a fish's spine. Each person in each car and each home had their own dramas to navigate. Sometimes they were joyous—another Tohler baby, for instance— and sometimes less happy. Life was full of drama.

I emerged from the woods into the clearing with the retreat center. A decade-old Kia was parked in the lot. Likely the stranger's. I put on my most confident smile and strolled up the stone patio to the door.

And stopped cold. Faint Spanish-inflected guitar music came from inside, and Wanda, oblivious to me or anything else, whirled a large fringed shawl around her. The silk wafted and whipped through the air while her feet tapped skillfully on the wooden floor. She was . . . flamenco dancing. And she was really good.

I was riveted. Wanda, with her stocky frame, denim work pants, and self-administered haircut, was far from an elegant Spanish beauty, but I couldn't wrench my eyes from her. Duke, her brother, was an accomplished dancer, too. He foxtrotted like a combination of Fred Astaire and Tweedledee. Maybe their parents had run a dance studio.

Through the window, Wanda waved her shawl at a nonexistent dance partner and snapped back her head, and I felt a twinge of sympathy. The partner who wasn't there was clearly all too real in her eyes.

Wanda's dancing slowed, and she dropped her arms. She'd seen me. She picked up her phone from a chair and cut the music.

I stepped inside. "You're an amazing dancer. I thought Duke was good, but you? Wow."

She nodded at the compliment. Only a faint sheen of moisture on her brow and neck showed her exertion at all. "Can I help you?"

I lifted the tote. "I'm here to refresh the library upstairs. Is the visitor in—the woman staying here a few days?"

"Don't know. I don't think so." She looped the shawl over her shoulder. "How was children's reading hour?"

"It went well." I'd heard kids laughing from Old Man Thurston's office while their caregivers drank coffee in the kitchen. "You can sit in on the next one, if you'd like. I bet Mona could use your help."

"That would be great. I've been thinking it over, and I'd like to focus my volunteer work on the children's collection, if that's all right with you." She affected that stiff smile again.

"Of course," I said.

"Terrific. Let me know if you need anything upstairs." She walked away, her heels clicking on the floorboards.

The retreat center's library filled two waist-high shelves on the upstairs landing. As soon as I plunked my tote bag in an armchair, the books on the shelves greeted me and said hello to the other books in the bag. Something I hadn't known until I came into my magic was how social books are. They like to be with readers, but second best was other books. Once I understood that, I knew why shelves full of books looked so much more content than a shelf with only a few novels and dusty knickknacks.

Wanda was downstairs, out of earshot. I knelt next to the shelves, hoping my magic wouldn't fail me. Despite the wavers this afternoon, it felt steadier now. "Books, has the visitor come to you?"

Yes, yes, they said in their harmony of voices.

"What did she choose?" Maybe something in her reading choices would tell me about her.

A few spines popped an inch from the others. I

pulled out the novel nearest me, a paranormal cozy, *Witch Hunt*, by Cate Conte. Interesting. *Practical Magic* by Alice Hoffman showed itself next. I sat back. A gap in the novels meant she must have taken another one to her room. Which one? *Witches* by Roald Dahl, came the whisper in my head.

Interesting. Witches fascinated the visitor. This was another possible link to Ian, who sold books about the paranormal.

"What is this about?" I said aloud.

"Did you say something?" came a woman's voice from behind me.

I whirled toward her, my heart skipping a beat. "No, nothing. Just muttering."

The woman closed her eyes, her chest rising with her breath. "They smell like vanilla, don't they? So calming. The books, that is."

I had to look twice. On the face of it, the stranger and I shared only a few similarities. We were both about the same age and build. But instead of a mass of red curls, she had straight chestnut brown hair braided and looped around her head. Her eyes were mossy green, not blue, like mine, and freckles dusted her face, while my freckles had vanished with childhood. My style was practical librarian. While also practical, her style looked artfully gathered from vintage clothing stores, giving her the vibe of Grace Kelly on a budget. Yet there was something familiar about her. I couldn't put my finger on it.

I stood. "I'm Josie Way, Wilfred's librarian. I was

just swapping out a few of the books. This is a sort of satellite library for visitors."

"Lise Bloom." Judging from her stare, she seemed fascinated by me, too. She broke her gaze with a glance toward the bookshelves. "Sorry I'm being rude. It's just that I feel like I've met you. Have you spent time in Astoria? That's where I live."

Astoria was a small town a few hours away, where the Columbia River met the Pacific Ocean. Sam and I had spent a weekend there once, walking the hills among the Victorian houses and strolling the waterfront eating fish and chips. We'd stayed at a hotel with a turntable and vinyl records, and Sam surprised me by knowing the lyrics to a Barry White album. Sam was no Wanda, but I could have danced with him all night. I didn't know if I had the heart to visit Astoria again. Not without him.

"A couple of days. That's it," I said. She might not live on the East Coast where Ian was from, but that didn't mean she wasn't a recent transplant. I wanted to ask her straight out why she was here in Wilfred, but it would seem too abrupt. Instead, I said, "Are you enjoying your time here?"

"Sure," she said, but didn't seem to pay attention to my response. Instead, she studied me.

What did she want? Perhaps she knew Ian was dating someone and wondered if I was his girlfriend. Or maybe I was totally wrong, and she was here to make etchings of lichen or write haikus.

"You must know people in town," I said, fairly certain she didn't—unless she knew Ian, that is.

"No."

"People have stayed here between retreats to medi-tate," I said. "Or hike."

"That sounds nice."

To heck with subtlety. I couldn't wait any longer. "What brings you to Wilfred, anyway?"

She examined me again. "Truthfully? I don't know."

Chapter Six

That night, as darkness fell, I finished my dinner of leftover pasta and pondered my interaction with Lise Bloom. How could she travel somewhere with no agenda? Some people were wanderers. But to spend days in Wilfred? It was scenic, sure, but there was nothing to do here except wander the woods. I finished washing my dinner plate and went to the living room. Rodney was already curled up in my armchair, his tail flicking.

My apartment abutted the atrium at the back of the house. At the right of the staircase was the entrance to my living room with its Victorian sofa and fireplace, and through that, my bedroom. Windows in both rooms looked over the lawn and oak trees to Big House.

Beyond my living room, two floors above the library's kitchen, was my own small kitchen and bathroom. If I turned left at the service stairwell instead of right, a short hall led to the open-air tower room.

I nudged Rodney aside and picked up my novel—

Death of a Peer by Ngaio Marsh—flipped through its yellowed pages, then rested it on my lap. I couldn't focus. The books had stopped speaking again, and my thoughts had thickened like molasses in January.

Then one voice pierced the library's quiet: my grandmother's. Her magic lessons called. Eagerly, I set my book aside and went to my bedroom.

I lit a beeswax taper. Rodney, purring, jumped to the bed and circled to make a nest in my quilt. I slid the green trunk from under my bed and let my hands sift through the sealed envelopes inside. Each envelope contained a message to me from my grandmother, a letter she'd written before she died and before I knew I was a witch. She'd foreseen I'd need a mentor. Every once in a while, as tonight, the letters asked to be read. Somehow I always chose the lesson I needed.

My fingers skimmed the letters until one warmed and seemed to move of its own volition to my palm. This was the one that held what I needed to know now. So much felt askew in my life. Would the lesson be about Sam? My heart ached at our distance. Or maybe about the lapses I'd felt in my magic. Or maybe a spell to find Ian.

I took the letter to bed. My curtains rustled in the night breeze, making a moving pattern of moonlight across the wood floor. Rodney crawled into my lap. This letter was fatter than the others.

I ripped open the envelope.

Dear Josie, I read. My grandmother's voice drifted from the pages and suffused me with warmth. I held the paper to my chest for a moment, enjoying the feeling. All at once, the warmth chilled. Not a good sign.

Rodney's purring ceased, and he looked up at me, his whiskey-tinted eyes wide. Slowly, I unfolded the letter.

> *Dear Josie,*
>
> *How I hoped you'd never read this letter. As I write, I hope it still. Perhaps this will be the envelope you never have to open. Perhaps this letter will stay cold and alone when all the others have been read and, I hope, have helped you become a strong, safe, and ethical witch.*
>
> *But here you are.*
>
> *Tonight—for I see it as night, perhaps summer, the breeze holding something more malevolent than sleepiness and the chirp of crickets—will not be a magic lesson. Instead, I write to you about power and an important chapter of our history.*
>
> *You are a moral person, Josie. I see it in you, even as a child. Your sense of justice infuses your worldview. You are outraged when your sister is bullied by a classmate and tearful to find a baby bird who didn't survive its maiden attempt at flight. Coupled with the force of your magic, this sense of justice can lead you to accomplish great things.*
>
> *It might also lead you into disaster. Since you are reading this letter, you must assume this is the case.*
>
> *Not everyone who is powerful is also just. Oh, I know this isn't news to you—or anyone—but knowing something and understanding it in your*

*bones are two different things. Experience makes
instinct of intellect.*

*In our bloodline of witches, you and I have
the mark of the most powerful. My grandmother
did as well, and I remember the star-shaped
birthmark on her shoulder showing when her
collar slipped as she rolled pie dough or dug in
the garden. Her gift was foresight, as is your
mother's. Combined with the force of her magic,
Nana could delve far into the future, the reach of
her abilities linked to the intensity of her vision.*

I paused to feel the birthmark on my shoulder heat
and tingle. I pressed a finger to it.

*One vision came to her repeatedly. As a little girl, I
heard her warning my mother not to have children
after I was born. I wasn't sure why. Would she die in
childbirth? My mother respected Nana's magic and
through the use of herbs and spells didn't conceive for
years. Until she did. My mother thought she'd passed
the time of life when she could have children, and she
let her monthly enchantments slip. In the meantime,
Nana died. I was nearly twenty when Beata was born.*

Here again, I paused, this time remembering my
mother mentioning Aunt Beata. I'd told her about my
lapses in magic, and she remembered this relative I'd
never heard of, an aunt who'd been banished from the
family. She couldn't tell me much, just that Beata existed and that some mystery surrounded her. At the

same time, Mom, who was visiting me at the time, was disturbed by Babe Hamilton, and it had crossed my mind they might be the same person. But I wasn't certain, and Babe and I had a good relationship. I had certainly never heard of Beata from my grandmother—until now, that is.

Outside my bedroom window, a crow cawed from the oak tree, and my breath quickened. I returned to my grandmother's words.

At first it seemed Nana must have been mistaken, for Beata—named because of the unexpected blessing she was—was a beautiful child. It was impossible to see her smile from her cradle and not fall in love with her. I certainly did. We all loved her. Grocery clerks let customers pile up so as to have a moment to stroke her golden hair. Rooms shushed in admiration when my mother walked in with Beata, holding her chubby toddler hand. Even mean dogs whimpered and wagged their tails in her presence.

When Beata was five years old, the birthmark surfaced on her shoulder. We didn't expect it. I had already inherited the mark, and it's unusual for two such powerful witches to be born the same generation. However, Beata was marked, and it was already clear her gift was glamour, the ability to charm you, make you see what she wanted you to see. It wasn't until she was older that her drive came to the surface. It wasn't

*healing, as is mine, or justice, as yours. No,
power drove her. The pure thrill of power—
seeing people bend to her, give to her, do what
she wanted—fed her life essence.*

Beata was a monster.

*She mastered her magic quickly and used it to
destroy families and drive formerly sober people
to excess. She could have anything she wanted.
If you wore a dress she fancied, you found yourself pressing it upon her with the belief you
didn't deserve it. She had to be the most loved
person in a room, which meant no husband was
safe. In our town, Beata was worshipped and
feared. She was absolutely drunk with power.
The more she had, the more she wanted, and she
didn't care who she ruined to get it.*

*I have to take a break here, darling. What I'm
about to write still burns as deeply as it did
when it happened so many years ago.*

Grandma's writing filled only half of the page. I set
it down and picked up the next. Rodney's steady purring comforted me. I didn't have my mother's gift of
foresight, but the tightness in my throat led me to dread
the words to come.

*You never knew your grandfather, but what a
wonderful man he was. He could build anything,
deconstruct any mechanical puzzle. And he was
kind. When I met him, it was as if I'd always
known him, as if I'd connected at last with the*

*part of me that would make me whole. He
accepted my magic as easily as he accepted my
habit of singing with the radio or taking early
morning walks. Oh Josie, I hope you have this
kind of love someday.*

Here I had to set down the letter again. *I had this love,
Grandma,* I thought. I had it and lost it. My gaze drifted to
the window. Sam's house was still dark. Where was he?

*You will suspect what happened next. Beata
couldn't stand my happiness. Not only did she
want it for herself, she wanted it taken from me.
I warned her to stay away from us, but it only
stoked her desire further. Your grandfather
began to act as a man possessed. He couldn't
sleep. He couldn't focus at work. No spell I cast
could protect him.*

*One afternoon he disappeared, Beata with
him. Three days later a motorist found him dead
in his truck at the bottom of a ravine. I believe
the struggle within him drove him from the road.*

*Beata glowed with victory. There was some-
thing else, too. I saw it in her eyes and sensed it
in the slight changes in her body. My years as a
healer made it as clear to me as the moon when
the sun sets. She was with child.*

*I had to stop her. Oh, I wouldn't stop her from
giving birth. I couldn't do that. But I couldn't let
her ruin a child's life, not to mention continue to
destroy the world around her. Her power needed
reined in. I didn't know if I had the magic to con-*

tain it, but I was the only person who might.
Fury and grief fueled my intention.

One night when the moon was full, I called
her to the garden. She admitted to seducing your
grandfather and, one hand on her belly, she
laughed at me. She actually laughed.

Summoning every fiber of magic within me
and within my garden, where over the years I'd
infused the roses and herbs and every other
plant with my energy, I cast a spell to contain
her magic and to banish her from our town.

Beata resisted. Of course she did. We fought
all night, throwing power against power. The sky
became like a lightning storm, and my garden
blackened to the ground.

In the end, I prevailed. At least, I did enough
that I never saw her again. Every once in a
while, however, I sense my sister. Some of her
magic must remain. She's out there. Somewhere.

Josie, my fear is she will appear in your life.
You are the only witch now alive with enough
power to break my spell of containment and re-
lease her full magic. If she can, she will find you,
and she will use what glamour she has to entrap
you. Be careful, my darling. Over the years she
will have honed what magic remains to a death-
sharp point. She will know you better than you
know yourself, and she will not hesitate to de-
stroy you.

I shiver as I write this, and I can only hope
your strength and goodness will overcome her.

All my love, Grandma

I shivered, too. I slipped from bed and pulled down the window.

Not long ago, I'd had a terrifying experience in the abandoned Empress Theater. My grandmother had materialized as a young woman on the mildew-splotched screen. She'd been casting a spell, and it had chilled me to the bone. Now I knew the spell was to banish Aunt Beata.

Beata was out there, and she planned to use me. But how?

Chapter Seven

I jolted awake. Dawn was still a few hours away. Something had disturbed me. Next to me, Rodney raised his head. I listened but heard nothing save the wind rustling the leaves of the cottonwoods by the river.

Normally I was a solid sleeper, and if I did wake, I luxuriated in the warmth of my bed and the knowledge that I was safe with nothing to do but let my mind wander while the world around me drowsed. Sometimes I summoned the books, and words that brought me comfort—say, Emily Dickinson's poems, or books I'd loved in childhood like *Ramona the Pest*—would read in soothing voices.

Tonight was different. The books were quiet. My breath quickened a notch. It wasn't that the books had nothing to say; it was that I couldn't hear them. Words garbled and muffled at the edge of my awareness, but nothing made it through. I sat up.

A thud sounded from downstairs, like a rucksack of firewood hitting the floor. Rodney jumped from beside me and went under the bed. I swung my legs from the covers just as the sound of crows cawing filled the night sky. My pulse beat double time.

I forced myself to open the door of my apartment and peer over the railing to the atrium. The moon was new, and I couldn't make out much from the scant light shining through the roof's stained-glass cupola. The portrait of Marilyn Wilfred over the front entrance was cloaked in darkness. Something black and sizable lay in the atrium—I thought it did, anyway.

"Hello?" I said, my voice wavering. "Is anybody there?"

I heard nothing but the relentless cawing of the crows. The books remained silent. Despite the summer night's heat, my skin prickled. I swallowed and turned for the service stairwell.

At ground level, the lump became clearer. It was a person, inert, lying on his side.

"Hello?" I ventured again. Nothing. Even the crows had stopped their shrieks.

I crept closer. A man, dressed in black, faced away from me. Did someone break in and fall—drunk, perhaps—on the floor? Gingerly, I edged around the form, keeping my distance in case he should leap up.

Now that I saw him, it was clear there would be no leaping up—not now, not ever.

I'd found Ian Penclosa at last. And he was dead.

Gasping, I backed away. I couldn't bear to stay in the atrium. Not with Ian's lifeless body staring up at me from the floor. Instead, I'd call the sheriff from the phone in my office. On my way, I glimpsed Sam's SUV through the window in the kitchen door. He was home.

This was better—more immediate—than calling. I ran across the garden between our houses and hurried up the steps to Sam's front porch. The door's beveled glass showed nothing but darkness. Natural at this hour.

I pounded on the front door. After a moment, light appeared in the hall's depths, light from upstairs. Then there he was. Sam, in hastily pulled-on jeans and a T-shirt, opened the door. I hadn't seen him in days, but I could deal with that later.

"It's Ian," I gasped.

"Slow down, Josie. What's this about Ian?"

I drew a shuddering breath. "I heard noise downstairs and went to check. I found Ian on the atrium floor."

"You said Ian is in the atrium?"

"Yes. Sam, he's . . . he's. . . ." I wanted to bury my face in his chest. Shivers wracked me. "He's dead."

Sam was all business. He grabbed his phone and led me back to the library. We went in the service door and crossed the old dining room to the atrium. He stopped short.

"Where?" he asked.

I couldn't look. "On the floor. Near the table where Lyndon puts the flowers."

"There's no one here." Sam's voice was cold.

My eyes flew open. "That can't be."

Yet it was. The place I'd seen Ian's body was empty. The atrium was still, silent. No body, no sign anyone had been there.

"I don't understand," I said. "I heard a noise, and I came downstairs. Ian has been missing for a few days. He was right here." I stood, uncomprehending, and stared at the floorboards.

Sam looked at me with an inscrutable expression, then shifted his gaze to the spot on the floor where I'd pointed. "There aren't any scuffs or marks here."

I could only nod dumbly.

"Ian uses a wheelchair. I don't see it." Sam popped into the kitchen and crossed to the foyer. In a moment, he was beside me again. "No wheelchair and no sign of one having come in."

"Maybe someone dumped his body." I couldn't think of any other explanation.

"And took it away again?" Sam stepped closer. "You say Ian has been missing?"

"Yes." A thousand thoughts whirled through my mind. "Lalena hasn't seen him for days. She asked me yesterday morning to try to find him."

I was sure I'd just seen Ian. Positive. Where had he gone?

"Wherever he is, he's certainly not here." Sam eyed me curiously. "You say you talked to Lalena about him?"

I nodded. Sam didn't believe me. I could tell.

"That's it, then. You were asleep and dreamed the whole thing."

"No. No, I tell you. I saw him." I should have taken a photo. I did see him. Didn't I? I breathed in and listened for the books. They would back me up. But they were silent.

I didn't want to look at Sam. I didn't want to see his look of pity—or worse.

"I'd better get home. Nicky is still sleeping."

I couldn't respond. Finally, I lifted my head and searched that face I loved so deeply, but I couldn't read it. He was thinking something, and he had something to say. He thought I was crazy, maybe. I'd told him I was a witch, and it was as if I'd ceased to exist. He hadn't replied to any of my calls or texts. He had cut me cold.

"Josie," he said at last. "Don't play with me."

Then he walked away.

Chapter Eight

The next morning at the library, I felt hungover, even though the strongest thing I'd drunk all week was coffee—this morning's coffee being especially powerful. I was bewildered and humiliated.

Last night after Sam left, I had checked the library's perimeter, testing locks and doors. Not one of them was open. There was no sign of entry, let alone Ian's wheelchair. Was Sam right, and I had hallucinated the whole thing? Yet I could close my eyes and see it all: Ian's black hair splayed under his head, the scar on his cheek especially white and waxy. The books had refused to let out even a murmur. Library patrons seemed to note my air of distraction and stayed away.

One name haunted my thoughts: *Beata*. Could she have had anything to do with last night's drama? If so, I couldn't figure out how or why. Each time I passed through the atrium, chills rumbled through my gut. As I'd noted last night, when my mother had visited a few weeks ago, she'd suspected Aunt Beata and Babe Hamilton were linked. That was a possibility. But what about Lise Bloom, the stranger at the retreat center? Something was oddly familiar about her, yet I was certain I'd never met her before yesterday. My urgency to find Ian intensified.

Just past noon, Lise Bloom came into the library. She stopped in the atrium to stare at the mansion's carved wooden moldings and three-story ceiling topped with a cupola—most newcomers did. I remembered my grandmother's warning about Beata. She could charm you into seeing whatever she wanted.

Wary but resolute, I joined her in the atrium. "You're still in town."

"Yes," she said. "I'm sorry for being so mysterious yesterday. I wanted to explain." She pointed to Marilyn Wilfred's portrait. "Who's that?"

I followed her gaze to the full-length painting over the entrance to the foyer. "That's the library's founder."

Marilyn stared down at us in a 1920s flapper gown. I'd always wondered if she had some sort of magic about her. Sometimes I swore she saw me and wrinkled her brow in warning or smiled with encouragement. Maybe the books' energy animated her. I didn't know—there was still a lot about magic I was learning.

"She looks alive, doesn't she?" Lise said. "Like she's ready to step from the painting. As if she's watching us."

I examined Lise Bloom again. A tremor of energy passed between us. *My Aunt Beata could appear to me as anything*, I reminded myself.

I was about to prompt Lise about her "mystery" when Lalena pushed her way through the front door with Sailor on a ribbon-leash behind her. She cast a brief glance at Lise, then laid a hand on my forearm. "Josie. We have to talk."

"Don't mind me," Lise said. "I'll have a look around." She wandered toward the conservatory.

Reluctantly, I let her go as Lalena pulled me into Old Man Thurston's former office, now Children's Literature. The oak-paneled room with its immense desk might have seemed an odd choice for kids' books, but somehow it worked. Instead of feeling foreboding, the stately paneling was cozy. Even the portrait of Thurston Wilfred over the mantel seemed to smile as if the town's children were his personal offspring. One of my favorite sights was Mona reading to a circle of toddlers, and one of my favorite sounds was the melody of circus music, kitten's mews, and chattering kindergartners the books sang to me. Today the books were silent.

I had no time to ponder that as Lalena gestured toward the desk and perched on its edge.

"It's Ian," she said. "He's still gone. It's worse, though." She dropped Sailor's leash, and he trotted out, surely to find Rodney. "Sam's asking around town about him."

"He is?" My heart skipped a beat as I realized Sam had at least taken me seriously enough to check in on Ian.

"Why? Why is the sheriff asking about Ian?" Lalena said.

I hedged. I couldn't tell her about seeing Ian's body. I had no proof it had been anything but a bad dream, and I didn't want to freak her out. I glanced toward the door to the atrium. Had Ian really been lying there, lifeless? Was he elsewhere, and I'd had some sort of vision? Or had I imagined the whole thing?

Fortunately, Lalena didn't pause for my response. "Something must be wrong with him." She chewed on a knuckle.

"What has Sam been asking?" I said.

She dropped her hand and turned her attention toward me. "He's back, Sam is. Oh, Josie, here I am going on about Ian. Has Sam talked with you?"

"Not about . . . not about us." The words felt barbed as they left my throat.

Lalena let a moment pass before speaking softly. "He's asking if anyone's seen Ian. That's all. I haven't been sleeping well, and I heard Sam knocking on Ian's door this morning. At the café, Darla told me he'd questioned a few of the regulars."

"You said Ian's attitude changed at about the same time construction started at the Empress. I know I asked you before, but is it possible he recognized someone from the construction crew?"

She shrugged. "He didn't say."

Sailor yapped from the atrium. Chances were that Rodney was teasing him by leaping through the banister on the main staircase to the atrium floor, or instigating a chase through Popular Fiction.

"Sailor!" Lalena called from the entrance to Old Man Thurston's office. "I'd better go get him." She turned to me. "You'll tell me if Sam says something, won't you?"

I nodded. I could only hope Sam would tell me anything.

Where was Ian, anyway? The books had no answers for me, not even a hint. I didn't know what was happening to Wilfred, to me, but my grandmother's warning burned in my mind.

I went on a search for Lise Bloom, but she was nowhere to be found. She must have left. I poked my head into the rooms upstairs but didn't find anyone except a high-school couple holding hands in Natural Science and Mrs. Garlington sorting sheet music in the organ room.

I slowly made my way back to the circulation desk. Something would happen; I felt it. Soon. Whatever it was, it would not be good.

Chapter Nine

Without further information to spur me to action, the most productive thing I could do was to relax and center myself. When the storm began to rise—for I was sure it would—I wanted to be ready. That evening, the patio at Darla's Café was as good a place as any to wind down.

The café was busier than usual, and the tavern door was propped open, letting out the chatter and laughter of a full house. Complementing the usual gathering of Wilfredians were many members of the crew working on the Empress. They were easy to pick out from their bright orange construction T-shirts and plaster-dusted work pants.

Darla filled my water glass. "What'll you have? We're out of the burgers."

"What's the special?" I asked.

"Salmon étouffée. We're out of that, too. Folks from the work down at the Empress are hungry tonight. How about a patty melt with tuna?"

"Sign me up," I said. "And an iced tea."

Darla left without jotting down my order. She never did write down orders but juggled them in her brain with the facility of a mainframe computer, never forgetting who couldn't stand pickles, was gluten-free, or routinely split their slice of peach pie with their wife.

Now that Sam had withdrawn from me, I felt especially alone. Tables were full of families. Across the patio, Buffy and Thor tucked into ice cream at a table with their grandmother, Patty. Duke and his housemate Desmond chatted amiably over pints of beer. Tohlers occupied two adjacent tables, playing cards and apparently finishing the last of the étouffée.

At least I could distract myself with a novel. The books would have foreseen this circumstance and hidden one away in my bag. I dug in my purse but came up dry. Not even a pamphlet. This disconnection with my magic was getting worse. What was going on? My grandmother's warning about Aunt Beata again rose to mind.

Darla returned with a glass of iced tea. "What were you doing out last night? It's not like you to wander around after dark. Montgomery spotted you headed toward the meadow."

"Out? I stayed in." All night. Thinking of seeing Ian's body in the atrium, I squeezed my eyes shut a moment.

A strident voice traveled the patio. Both Darla and I looked up to see Wanda a few tables away, leaning toward Ruth Littlewood.

Ruth Littlewood, Wilfred's champion bird watcher and a library trustee, fondled the ever-present binoculars dangling from her neck. Before she retired, she ran a vegetable canning operation. These days she used her executive skills in natural history, researching local wildlife habits and updating her bird list.

"*Puss in Boots*," Wanda said. "Can you believe it?"

I couldn't make out Ruth's response.

Darla returned her attention to me. "I'm sure I saw you last night. Montgomery did, too. You were strolling up the Magnolia like you were on your way somewhere important. Montgomery thought you were stopping at Lalena's, but you kept going." Seeing my blank look, she added, "I guess we were mistaken." She left to take another table's order.

I steadied my breath. So far, my plans to relax were not gaining traction. Maybe Darla had seen Lise Bloom. At a distance, we might be mistaken for each other. Lise might have taken a shortcut through the trailer park to return to the retreat center.

"It isn't right." Wanda's voice carried.

Cats clearly upset Wanda. I wasn't sure how happy she'd be volunteering at the library with Rodney roaming the premises, but one thing was sure: if the choice was between Wanda or Rodney, the cat stayed.

Wanda's stiletto gaze in my direction let me know she'd marked my presence. Ruth turned, too, and shook her head. Ruth, keeping her gaze on me, said something under her breath to Wanda.

All I wanted was peace and quiet. No—no, that wasn't right. I wanted Sam's company and the murmuring of the books. Both had been inexplicably ripped from me. Did I have enough magic without them to discover why? At least I could sit at home with Rodney in my lap and eat dinner in peace. I'd get my patty melt to go.

I scanned the patio for Darla, and my eyes lit on a spiffily dressed man with a charming smile, the man I'd seen arguing with the construction worker the night before last.

To my surprise, he crossed the patio and placed a palm on the chair next to mine. "You're the librarian here, aren't you? May I sit with you? The other tables are taken."

I stood and stuck out a hand. "Josie Way."

"Josie Way, what do you say to a drink in the tavern?" He tossed his head toward Wanda and Ruth's table. "Don't ask me why, but we're getting the stink eye. We might find it more peaceful inside."

He was generous to pretend their glances were for anyone but me alone. Darla would bring my dinner into the tavern. I'd talk later to Wanda about Rodney and her fear of cats. "I'd like that."

Darla's Café was split into three zones: the patio, the café proper, and the tavern. On summer evenings, the patio was where I preferred to be, as did the rest of Wilfred. At dusk, the crickets chirped in the meadow, and Darla had planted pots of black-eyed Susans that glowed under the lights strung on the patio's awning. The café itself, with its black-and-white checkerboard floor and utilitarian booths, was my favorite spot for a breakfast of Darla's shrimp and grits and an earful of town gossip.

The tavern, however, rarely tempted me. It was a

boxcar-like addition to the café you could enter through the parking lot or through a red-padded door from the dining room. Passing from the café to the tavern was like crossing the border to a different country. You went from the café's bright cheer and aroma of bacon and waffles to a dark, beer-scented cave with the TV tuned to sports. Despite Oregon's longtime smoking ban and Darla's many air fresheners, the faint stink of cigarettes as old as the Nixon administration lingered in the ancient indoor-outdoor carpeting.

Tyrone and I found a booth not far from the bar. "You seem distracted," he said.

"I am, a bit," I replied. Tyrone was too model-perfect to attract me, but those warm brown eyes and smile encouraged me to talk.

"I don't blame you, what with those ladies staring at you. What's their deal?"

Orson, casting a curious glance from Tyrone to me, slid a platter with my patty melt and fries in front of me. "Anything for you?" he asked Tyrone.

"A beer, please. Whatever you have on tap."

Orson returned to the bar, and I dug into my dinner. "Strangely, I think it has to do with cats."

"That's a good one. Tell me more."

"One of the women, Wanda, seems really uncomfortable around the library's cat. She even took offense to *Puss in Boots*, the book for children's hour this week. She's a new volunteer at the library." I made an exaggerated frown. "And she shows up tomorrow for her first shift. I'm afraid she's going to want me to shut out the cat."

"I know how to handle that," Tyrone said. "*The Cat in the Hat*. Put it face-out."

"Or T. S. Eliot's *Old Possum's Book of Practical Cats*." I couldn't help but smile. I was already feeling better. I remembered Wanda dancing at the retreat center, swinging her fringed shawl so gracefully at the partner who wasn't there. "I think Wanda's lonely. She's new in town and hasn't made many friends." *Except Ruth*, I thought. "Her brother lives here, but he's busy."

"You have my sympathy. People like her, you have to draw a line, or they'll run you down. I know what I'm talking about. Let's not give her any more of our attention. Tell me about you."

For the next half hour, Tyrone and I talked. He told me about books he liked—he wasn't much of a reader, but lately he'd been interested in the stoic philosophers. He was staying at the Wallingford Guest House and had come to Wilfred from somewhere out east.

"I wanted a new start," he said. "I haven't been here long, but Wilfred is a sweet little place."

"I used to live near Washington, D.C.," I told him. "Worked at the Library of Congress. I came to Wilfred to get away from Washington and discovered I loved it here. Small-town life has its advantages."

Tyrone's gaze lost focus. He shook his head as if to shake away a memory. "You ever think of how much of life is chance? You just do the next thing, then the next thing, as if life is a river and you're on a raft with no rudder." He pushed away his empty beer glass. "I'm through with that. I want to be more purposeful with what I do with my life. Instead of running *from,* I want to be running *toward*."

"I get that." Escaping Washington had awoken not only my magic, but my entire life. I would always be a librarian—I loved books too much not to be, and besides, I was good at it. But I could also use my skills to pursue justice. In the past few years, for the first time, I felt in control of my life. My thoughts veered toward my freaky lapses in magic and the specter of Ian's body on the atrium floor. Almost in control, that was.

"I got caught up in the idea that you had to have money to be worth anything, that respect was about the nice car and the fancy watch." Tyrone smiled widely and lifted a palm to wave at Candace from the Beauty Palace.

Candace tossed her hair and returned his smile. She took a seat at the bar. Looking over her shoulder at Tyrone, she smiled again.

Tyrone was popular with the ladies, that was for sure. I had the feeling he'd been piloting that particular boat in life's river just fine. As charming as Tyrone was, I would take Sam over him any day. Tyrone's strong jaw and melting eyes were nothing next to Sam's intense gaze and eccentric habits. Advertising had it that a person had to look like Barbie or Ken to inspire love. Truth was, when you loved someone, the tiniest detail— a goofy smile, a receding hairline, a habit of snapping fingers when remembering something—became a draw far more alluring than perfect teeth.

That said, it was nice to talk with a handsome man and to feel appreciated as a woman—and a friend. I wouldn't say no to another drink with him sometime.

"It takes courage to change your life's course like that," I said.

"If you only knew." Tyrone's voice was quiet.

Whatever this change he was gearing up for, it was important to him. Following his gaze to the bar, I determined that this diversion in course was perhaps less important than his immediate goal. I'd leave him to talk with Candace. The barstool next to hers was open, and she tossed a flirtatious look Tyrone's way. Tyrone nodded toward her.

"Thank you for the conversation." I rose and slung my purse over my shoulder. "I've got something I need to do at home. See you around."

Tyrone drew his attention back to me. "See you later, Josie. It was great talking with you. Don't let the anti-cat lady get you down."

Chapter Ten

The summer night was as warm and soft as silk velvet. I pushed open my bedroom window and tried to avert my eyes from Big House, but I couldn't help but check to see if Sam's SUV was there. It was. Yellow light escaped from the crack in his bedroom curtains. He was so close, yet so far.

A crow alit on the roof of the gable below me and sharpened his beak on the roof tiles.

Chills shivered through me as I turned away from the window. I had to get to the bottom of what hampered my magic. I had a handful of clues: Babe Hamilton; Ian's disappearance; Lise.

A dark force sought to bind my magic by severing my connection to books. Maybe that force was also responsible for my seeing Ian's body. I was forced to admit Sam had been right. Ian couldn't have made it into the library without his wheelchair, and there had been no sign of that. Until now, the interfering magic had been relatively minor, but it seemed to be gathering force. I had to figure out who and what was behind it.

Scrying was the best way I knew to piece them together. In brief, scrying was using a reflective surface—a crystal ball, a mirror, a slab of polished obsidian, even a bowl of water—to see images. Sometimes these images concerned the future, but foresight wasn't my gift. I simply wanted to know what was happening to me now.

I pulled a fresh beeswax taper from a drawer and lifted a heavy brass candlestick from its place on the end table. I tucked *Grimm's Fairy Tales* under my arm. Since I was a child, I'd loved this book. Because I'd put so much energy into these stories over the years, their words had fueled some of my most powerful spells. I needed *Grimm's Fairy Tales* and the powers of the rest of the library's books to fuel my magic, if I could wrest it free.

Rodney trotted down the stairs behind me. The books, which would normally be stirring into a wave of sound, barely let out a buzz. The whispers I could make out sounded strained. I hoped I could rally enough magic to make scrying work at all.

I hesitated at the center of the atrium. This was, after all, where I'd seen Ian's body. Here, in the dark, as tonight. However, what repulsed me from the memory was also why I wanted to scry here. If someone else's magic was involved, its residue might linger. I lit the candle and set it in the atrium's middle, where moonlight through the cupola's stained glass splashed red,

green, and blue light. Rodney lay on his side, with a
spill of green on his fur, and lazily blinked at me.

From the kitchen I brought a bowl of water and placed
it near the candle so its flame would illuminate the
water's surface. Following my grandmother's instruc-
tions, I cast a protective circle large enough to hold me
and Rodney.

The library around me was oppressively quiet. Oh,
how I hoped the scrying would work. I could feel my
senses dulling, as they'd been before the spell binding
my magic had been released a few years earlier. I
couldn't go back to that way of living. Not now, when
afternoon skies were so vivid, food tasted so good, the
wind smelled of the earth, and I knew love.

"Books," I whispered, half craving, half fearing their
response. "Books, lend me your energy to see what
stands between me and my magic."

I felt as if I were inside a bubble with transparent yet
viscous walls. Energy pushed against those walls, but
it might have been outside the library altogether, its
force was so weak.

"Books," I pled, "please. Speak to me."

Magic's force continued muffled, faraway. Rodney
stood suddenly and growled, looking into the darkness.

"Hush, baby. We're safe here."

I saw nothing, heard nothing. I picked up the blue-
bound volume of *Grimm's Fairy Tales*. I held the book
to my chest and breathed deeply. Then I ruffled my fingers through its pages until a tingle told me *here*. I set
the book in my lap and opened it where my fingers had
landed. My heart fell.

To accompany the scrying, *Grimm's Fairy Tales* had selected "The Old Witch," a particularly gruesome tale. However, if this was the cost for gathering magic, I'd pay it. I read the story's beginning:

> There once was a little girl who was very obstinate and willful, and who never obeyed when her elders spoke to her; so how could she be happy?

The story was short, merely a page. I read on. The story related how the stubborn girl insisted on visiting an evil old witch who could appear in many guises, but whose true face was "a creature with a fiery head." The story ended with the witch changing the girl into a block of wood and tossing her on the fire.

Warning received. I closed *Grimm's Fairy Tales*.

The water's surface rippled on the bowl I'd set next to the candle. Slowly, I rested my hands on the book of fairy tales so not to disturb the magic I'd managed to squeeze from it. I softened my vision, and I stared at the bowl and let images unfurl.

When scrying, it wasn't as if I watched a movie on the water's surface. Instead, the ripples swirled and sparked pictures in my head. The first image was all ivory with pale brown spots, like a pony. No, it was skin. Lise Bloom's freckled skin. But no Lise Bloom. That image faded to black.

Then a fresh ripple on the bowl's surface brought to mind sheets hung outside to dry and flapping in the wind. My chest tightened. Babe Hamilton. She sold linens and had told me how she laundered vintage cotton carefully and hung it outside to dry so the sun would bleach it and the scent of the grass freshen it. I caught a glimpse of hands fastening a clothespin to the line. The hand was soft and young. Babe was likely in her sixties now, with blue veins showing beneath her pale skin.

The last image quickly coalesced into a crow. Again, Rodney growled and leaned back, the fur on his tail puffing. First, I saw one crow, then another, then several, until the bowl was black with them. I stood suddenly. *Grimm's Fairy Tales* dropped from my lap, knocking over the bowl.

I flattened a palm over my racing heart and forced my breathing to slow.

Babe Hamilton was involved with the trouble with my magic. I didn't know exactly how, but I could certainly find out why.

I spent a restless night pondering the waning of my magic and feeling the nearness yet distance of Sam, barely a hundred feet from my bedroom window. Despite my lack of sleep, I rose from bed the next morning with purpose. Today I would be calling on a witch.

That is, maybe I'd be calling on a witch. Babe had always been someone I could relax with, chat with as if she were a friend. She shared my love of beautiful textiles, I thought, as I folded back the quilt on my bed. It was a dizzying pattern of pieced vintage fabric, and sleep—usually—came easily under its soft warmth.

But wasn't that how glamour was? The ability to appear however someone wanted you to appear? If, as my grandmother had warned, Beata was a master at glamour, even with most of her magic cut away, she might still wield enough to appear as Babe. I'd have to rely on my instincts to feel this one out.

A cup of coffee later, I was on my way to the Magnolia Rolling Estates with Rodney prancing ahead. Sam's SUV was gone for the day. I'd heard his engine as I dressed, but it didn't make passing his empty driveway any easier.

I'd tucked the *Grimm's Fairy Tales* into my bag. It might be more of a talisman than a source of power now, but its presence comforted me. The whole library had been quiet this morning, and my world was beginning to dim. I had to get my magic back before it vanished completely. My plan was to confront Babe and to keep my senses alert for any magical tremor. I would use surprise to my advantage.

At the Magnolia Rolling Estates, most of the residents were still asleep. Lalena would be in bed for at least a few more hours, and Ian's trailer had the dead look of a home that hadn't been lived in for a while. I couldn't hear the books as I passed. Darla's trailer was lit, and Montgomery passed before the kitchen window. Darla would have been up for hours and was almost certainly at the café now, brewing coffee and mixing pancake batter.

However, Babe was an early riser. She'd often told me how it gave her the advantage at the estate sales where she sourced vintage linens. Her trailer's curtains were drawn, but the kitchen window glowed through its voile covering. She was awake. I looked down to tell Rodney to wait for me outside, but he'd disappeared. I was on my own.

I didn't think too much—I simply knocked on Babe's door, my knuckles sounding sharp against the metal.

Steps; another light coming on; the door opened. Babe's face was pale through the screen. "Josie?" The screen door creaked as she opened it. In a bathrobe and without a face of makeup and her signature red lipstick, Babe looked older than I'd assumed. "Is everything okay?"

All at once, my resolve melted. What had I been thinking? The *Grimm's Fairy Tales* in my bag let out a faint shiver and faded. I was here for a reason, I reminded myself. "May I come in? It's early, but I figured you'd be up."

"Of course." She stepped aside to let me pass.

Roz had rented the trailer to Babe when she'd moved in with Lyndon, but few traces of her remained. The plaid-upholstered sofa was Roz's, but I hardly recognized it draped with antique kanthas. Bits of hand-tatted lace covered the windows beneath Roz's oatmeal-hued curtains. A cheerful 1950s cotton tablecloth covered the kitchen table, with images of baskets bursting with plums, strawberries, and bananas. A stack of linens sat on one of the chairs. She must have been sorting them for the shop when I knocked.

This was not the home of a witch out to steal my power. This was where a tired middle-aged woman lived who made her living rummaging through people's castoffs and selling what she'd salvaged. She was no femme fatale. Why had I come here, anyway? I felt so tired. Maybe when I returned home, I could nap a few minutes before opening the library. Without asking, I took an armchair. My tote bag fell to my side.

"Can I get you a cup of coffee?" Babe asked.

"Yes, please. The cup I had seems to have worn off."

Babe poured from a percolator and splashed cream into the mug. Both the percolator and mug must have come from estate sales—they looked lifted straight from a black-and-white TV sitcom.

Babe set my mug on the side table and lowered herself to the couch. "What's wrong, honey?" She leaned forward, not in prurience, but in concern. "Does this have to do with Sam?"

The shiv of pain from thinking of Sam prompted me to speak. "Are you my Aunt Beata?"

Mouth agape, Babe fell back into the couch. "Your *what*?"

From her puzzled expression, I knew I'd been mistaken. What had I been thinking? Before me sat a normal woman, drained by the early hour and definitely free of magic's sparkle. How could I suspect her responsible for the waning of my magical abilities, not to mention the force behind the crows that followed me and the dozens of other strange occurrences? Babe stared at me as if I'd lost my mind. Maybe I had.

I shook my head. "Sorry. I've been . . . I've been under a lot of strain lately."

"I understand." Her voice was soft. "Sometimes life can take odd turns. Not everyone is meant for us. Someday you'll look back and understand why this happened."

She was thinking of Sam. Like everyone else in town, she'd noticed our distance, and she was kind enough to take a motherly approach. My throat thickened.

"Who is this aunt . . . Aunt Beatrice?" she asked.

"Beata. Aunt Beata. My mother was telling me about her. She's been on my mind, and I thought . . . I wondered. . . ." I couldn't think of a way to wrap up my thoughts. "Sorry for busting in on you like this."

"Never mind. I'm glad you stopped by." She stood. "I would have come up to the library today to see you, anyway. I found something you should have."

Babe pulled a sheet from the stack of linens on the kitchen chair. She set it on my lap. Time had dimmed to ivory the sheet's thick cotton-linen blend, and many washings had softened the fabric. "For me?"

"Yes. Look." She pointed to the initials embroidered into its top edge surrounded by vines and smooth, deco-inspired dots in glossy cotton thread. *J. W.* My initials. "I thought of you right away."

I ran my palm over the fabric. So beautiful. "I didn't bring my purse."

"Darling, please. It's a gift." She patted the sheet and stood. "Beauty is comfort. Get it where you can. Besides, you've been a good customer."

"I can't thank you enough, Babe."

She pulled me into a motherly embrace. "Don't worry about Sam. Things will turn out how they're meant to."

"It's not just that." As true as my words were, my voice was unconvincing.

"Don't worry about Ian, either, honey. Now, have a good day, and we'll talk soon."

It wasn't until I was almost all the way home that I wondered, *How did she know about Ian?*

Chapter Eleven

Babe Hamilton wasn't my Aunt Beata. Seeing her so drab and bereft of her usual charm had convinced me she didn't have it in her to lasso my magic. I hadn't felt the slightest magical tingle in her presence. If not her, then who?

It was hard to focus that day at the library. The crow that followed me home from Babe's had added another layer of worry. He'd perched on my bedroom window's sill and winged off only when Rodney had hissed at him.

When Maury Johanssen asked me for a recommendation for a western with a strong romantic subplot, normally four or five titles would have leapt to mind. Instead, I was reduced to searching my memory, then turning to the internet. When Ashley Pitt stopped by the circulation desk to see if I knew any good books about winter farming, I drew a similar blank.

My thoughts turned to Ian. Could he be stealing my magic? He was mysterious, that was for sure, and he held a deep interest in the occult. I cringed at the memory of his body in the atrium and my call to Sam. Glamour might have easily transformed him from Beata, and his appearance here, in the middle of the night, could have been a play to weaken me. If so, it had worked.

Then there was Lise, the stranger. She was somehow familiar. Perhaps it was a blood link. Maybe she was Aunt Beata. She had no good explanation for staying in Wilfred.

A rap on my desk disturbed my pondering. Mona—no foster animal with her this time—leaned close.

"Did you see them?" she said in a low voice.

"Who?"

She gestured toward Old Man Thurston's office across the atrium. "Wanda and Ruth. They're in the children's room, making notes."

Wanda wasn't due to start her shift as a library volunteer for another hour. "Notes about what?"

"That's just it—I don't know. They're being really mysterious. I tried to look, but Ruth tipped the notebook against her chest so I couldn't see."

Remembering Wanda and Ruth's confab at the café, I pushed myself away from the desk. If it were Wanda alone, I'd assume she was getting familiar with the library and ignore it, but Ruth Littlewood was a library trustee. I needed to know what she was up to. I crossed the atrium to Children's Literature, Mona behind me.

"Hello Ruth, Wanda," I said. "Can I help you with anything?"

"No, Josie," Ruth said. "We're doing just fine, thank you." She set a sheet of paper on a chair. It was half-full of some sort of entries, but I couldn't make out details.

"It's not time to meet yet, is it?" Wanda asked. She stood facing me in front of a shelf, but kept a finger wedged between two books, as if she were marking her place.

"No," I said. "Are you looking for a particular book? I could search online for you." Back when my magic was at its peak, all I'd have to do was let my mind relax, and titles would fill it. Not now.

"As I said," Ruth said, her tone of voice making clear that the subject was concluded, "we're doing fine."

Just then, a blur of black fur rocketed through Old Man Thurston's office, snatched the sheet of paper Ruth had set on the chair, and tore through to the atrium.

"Rodney!" I yelled after him. Too late. He moved too fast for me to stop him. The paper was gone for good. "I'm so sorry. I hope it wasn't important."

"Point in case," Ruth said.

"Point in case what?" I asked.

"Nothing." Wanda clenched a smile so hard, I feared for her molars. "Nothing at all."

That night I continued to feel as if a noose were tightening around me. I wandered my apartment—out the tiny kitchen, down the hall overlooking the atrium, into my living room, and through to my bedroom—only to repeat the pacing in the opposite direction.

Ian was still missing. Lalena had sent me several mournful texts, but she didn't want my company, and I didn't have the right words to soothe her.

And then there was the obliteration of my magic. I dropped to my bed, spurring Rodney to emerge from his dark napping place under it. He leapt to my side. At least he was still with me, but for how long? Whatever the dark magic was, and from wherever it came, it was getting worse. My power was locked up, and the walls around it grew thicker. I'd been so sure I'd seen Ian's body in the atrium. I winced at the memory. Was that part of the dark magic, too?

Another thing I had to contend with was Wanda's seeming phobia about Rodney. It wasn't just me who loved having him at the library. Patrons had told me scores of times how they enjoyed finding him napping in the cookbook section or batting a pencil down the hall or simply stretched on a windowsill enjoying the view.

I resisted looking out the windows. Either Sam was home and refusing to spend time with me, or he was away and I'd wonder where he was, and with whom. Either way was another twist to my heart.

I lay back, and Rodney climbed onto my chest. "Naughty cat," I told him. "Where did you hide Ruth Littlewood's list, anyway?"

As I talked, I stretched, and my fingers touched the embroidered monogram on the sheet Babe Hamilton had given me.

I sat abruptly, dumping Rodney to the side. I pulled the monogram closer and examined it. The thread was a shade lighter than that used for the rest of the embroidery. It was newer. As I fingered the fabric, my senses grew even more dull. Dread rippled through my torso.

No. Couldn't be. I leaned back and took in the pattern as a whole, and I saw it: a glyph.

My grandmother's letters had taught me about glyphs. They were spells made by a word or phrase written out with repeating letters eliminated. The remaining letters were then fashioned into a symbol embodying the intent and energy of the person who'd made the glyph. In short, my sheet carried a spell. Because the spell was made of words—my magical source—it would pack even greater power.

It had been Babe Hamilton all along. Babe was a witch. Babe was draining me of my magic, trapping me in a deadening bubble. Babe was my Aunt Beata.

I leapt away from the sheet, then tore it from the bed, dumping my blankets on the floor. I could barely catch my breath. What else had I bought from her?

The quilt, for one. Touching only corners, I dragged it and the sheet to the landing outside my living room door. I'd purchased at least two more sheets from Babe. I pulled them, freshly washed and folded, heavy from vintage métis, from the linen closet and tossed them on the others. I had no idea if they were enchanted, too, but I wasn't taking chances.

What else? I ransacked the kitchen drawer where I kept dishtowels and cloth napkins and added four dishtowels and a napkin embroidered with four-leaf clovers to the pile growing on the landing. A 1920s chemise threaded with pink ribbon. A rustic linen table runner with poppies on it. A length of handmade lace.

My heart throbbed double time in my chest, and my hands trembled. Did I have enough magic left to fight hers? I had to try.

Chapter Twelve

Finally, it was late enough to carry out my task. I'd tied the linens into the largest sheet and stuffed a tote bag with salt, matches, lighter fluid, and my volume of *Grimm's Fairy Tales*. It barely spoke to me now, but it contained all the magic I had left.

I set out quietly into the night. Both Big House and the caretaker's cottage were dark, and it was late enough that the air had cooled and the crickets ceased their chirping. Only the whoosh of the wind in the cottonwoods on the river's bank broke the complete silence.

Then I heard it: the faraway caw of a crow.

My breath quickened, but nothing would get in the way of what I had to do now. Rodney on my heels, I circled the library and followed the path along the river until I could turn off to a less-used trail going into the woods. Here, sure no one could see me, I flicked on my flashlight.

The dark of the forest nearly swallowed the shaft of light, and the moon, now just a sliver, was little help.

"Slow down, kitty," I urged Rodney.

He knew where we were headed: to the witch's circle. Most often when I wanted to practice magic best carried out outdoors, I went to the abandoned stacking house on the other side of the retreat center, near the millpond. The concrete stacking house's roof had long fallen in, and its windows and doors had rotted decades ago. Trees sprang up in its crevices, and it had the feeling of a plein air cathedral. I loved it.

However, the stacking house was too close to the retreat center for me to burn anything larger than a taper. The last thing I needed was the volunteer fire department showing up as I was setting fire to a pile of cotton and linen. I shook my head, trying to imagine explaining that.

An owl hooted from somewhere near. At least it wasn't a crow. Something rustled in the underbrush, and I shivered. Besides these noises, all I heard was my own breath as I steadily made my way over roots and through the knee-high ferns to the witch's circle. A few minutes later, I thought I'd made a wrong turn and veered too far west, but soon I found the opening in the trees.

Here I was at last. I dropped my tote to my feet and caught my breath. The witch's circle was a meadow the size of a suburban backyard, but it was large enough that moonlight, as thin as it was, iced the grass and mossy logs. Fir trees surrounded us like mammoth sentries.

I'd accidentally stumbled upon the circle the summer before, when I was gathering mushrooms with a friend who was in Wilfred as part of a team to film an interview with Roz about her bestseller, *The Whippoorwill Cries Love*. The friend, Leo, was also researching a documentary on folk magic. He'd pointed out the clearing and told me they were considered magical places, both feared and venerated. I cared less about that and more about the fact that I was far enough from the trail that I wouldn't be seen.

I clicked off my flashlight. Within twenty minutes, I'd gathered enough rocks to construct a rough fire pit. I inhaled deeply to center myself, then pulled out my salt canister—no fancy silk pouch of sea salt, but it would do—and poured a circle a few feet outside the rocks. This would be my sphere of protection. As the salt's trail disappeared into the earth, I whispered a spell of safety, and my birthmark burned with the spark of magic. No dark forces would reach me here. Nothing that wasn't already here, that was. The pile of linens now rested in a crumpled heap in the fire circle's center.

"Here goes, Rodney."

Rodney mewed a long meow that stretched into the night. He wasn't often a vocal cat, espousing the view that actions spoke louder than words, but he had something to say now.

I laid the kindling over the sheet-wrapped bundle of linens, dumped lighter fluid on it, and lit a match.

The flame tightened into a black spiral, like a tiny tornado, and for a moment I feared it wouldn't catch. The night was completely silent—I knew it was—yet the screaming of crows pierced my eardrums. I covered them with my hands and screwed my eyes shut.

Then I felt the birds in my hair, pulling, pecking, screeching, but when I went to swat them away, nothing was there.

I pulled *Grimm's Fairy Tales* to my chest and willed whatever magic I had left to come to me. Through the deafening shrieks of the crows, the book dared a few words, "Our Lady's Little Glass." This was one of my favorite stories and only a paragraph long. When I was a little girl, I begged my mother to read it to me again and again—its simple ending soothed me. I recited the story's closing lines by heart:

Then Our Lady plucked a little white flower
with red stripes, called bindweed, which looks
very like a glass, and gave it to the wagoneer. He
filled it with wine, and then Our Lady drank it,
and in the self-same instant the cart was set free
and the wagoneer could drive onwards.

The crows' crying fell away. At the same time, the bundle caught, and flames leapt high. The linens were burning, blue sparks dancing above them. With each second that passed, I felt as if chiffon-thick layers of oppression were lifting and dissolving, drifting up with the smoke.

I woke to the night at last. The air smelled of dried pine needles and earth, and patches of warmth from the fire and chill from under the protective boughs of the fir trees drifted over me. I was lighter. The shackles on my magic burned away with the fabric, and I smiled, then laughed, when I realized I could hear books again.

Grimm's Fairy Tales was positively chatty. Rumpel-stiltskin, Sleeping Beauty, and Hansel and Gretel all clamored for my attention.

"I hear you," I told them, so happy I could barely choke out the words.

The fire burned strong. Beyond the smoke, the stars shone crisp. Two shooting stars, one right after the other, sailed over me like flaming arrows, vanishing into the night.

Babe Hamilton. She had come to Wilfred and set up shop, waiting, because she wanted to use me. She watched me through crows. She used glamour to shield her identity. My grandmother had warned me about Beata, and here she was.

As the linens burned to ashes, my magic poured back into me. I felt it in my body as a thrumming current, but I also knew it from the intensity of the colors and smells suffusing the night woods. I was free. My magic had been restored. Whatever it was Beata wanted, I felt more than ready to face it head-on.

Chapter Thirteen

Despite my late night, I woke up invigorated. I threw back the covers and rushed to the landing outside my living room, overlooking the atrium.

"Good morning, books!" I shouted.

Their greetings streamed from every room: high-pitched *hello*s from Children's Literature; the trumpeting of elephants from Natural History; *guten tag* from Foreign Language; and, from Music, Grieg's melody from *Peer Gynt*, "Morning Mood." It was a beautiful morning, indeed. The spell was broken. Everything was sweeter. Sure, I'd have to be wary. I couldn't let down my guard around Babe/Beata, but I was more than prepared to deflect whatever she dealt me.

I couldn't wait to help patrons choose their reading. The books would brim with recommendations. More than that, now that my magic was on board and energy back, I would have even more ability to help Lalena track down Ian.

As I circled the library, opening curtains and turning

on lights, I made a plan. First, I'd check with Lalena to see if she'd been in touch with Ian since yesterday or if she had any fresh ideas of where he might be. If she didn't have leads, I'd get back in touch with the construction manager at the Empress.

Then there was Lise Bloom. She was a recent arrival to Wilfred, too, and despite having no obvious business here, she kept hanging around.

All the time, of course, I'd need to steer clear of Babe Hamilton. The glyphs—her spells—had been potent enough to hamper me as long as I didn't know about them, and her glamour was strong enough to seduce me into a friendship and to mistake her as benign. However, I'd been able to break the spells fairly easily once I'd found their source.

My grandmother had bound the greater part of her sister's magic, but not all of it. As long as Grandma's spell held and I guarded against her, Babe-slash-Beata would not be able to hurt me. Or so I hoped.

When her spells collapsed, Babe may have sensed her magic returning to her, deflected from me. I hoped she would acknowledge defeat and leave Wilfred. Until then, I'd do my best to avoid her.

I returned to my apartment to lock up and found Rodney in my living room, sitting on a pile of shredded paper. "What is it, kitten? Have you turned gerbil?"

I picked up a shred and laughed despite myself. It was Ruth's notes from the other day, now completely illegible.

Rodney was feeling good today, too.

*   *   *

Buoyed by the return of my magic, I settled at the circulation desk. A woman trailing two boys was the first patron. I awaited the books' recommendations of adventure stories, but instead, one title floated into my brain: *Mindfulness for Anger Management*.

"May I help you?" I asked.

"I want to make a formal complaint," the woman said.

"Please." I motioned toward a chair. "Have a seat. Tell me what's on your mind."

The older boy slouched into the chair, instead, and pulled out a phone to play a video game. The younger boy, probably just old enough to read, wandered toward the atrium.

Their mother leaned over my desk. "It's the person you have working in the kids' room."

"Mona?"

"No. Someone else. Short, stocky. Smiles a lot."

Wanda. "She's a new volunteer. She doesn't know the books very well yet."

The woman shook her head. "It's not that. My son found a story he wanted to check out, and the volunteer told him he shouldn't read it, that it wasn't good for him."

"What book was it?" News in the library world was rife with stories of censorship. Everything from Anne Frank's *The Diary of a Young Girl* to *The Handmaid's Tale* had been challenged. So far, no one in Wilfred had issues with our book selection. The biggest complaints I'd received were about the coffee—some patrons liked French roast, and others preferred something lighter.

"Pete the Cat," the woman said.

"I'm sorry," I said. "Did you say *Pete the Cat*?"

"Yes. We have a cat named Pete, so my son was really excited when he saw the book. Then this lady tells us we're making a mistake. What's that about?"

Instead of replying what I thought, which was *I have no freaking idea*, I calmly said, "I see. Thank you for telling me. I'll have a word with her."

Wanda had a drawer in Old Man Thurston's desk for her library files. I taped a note to its outside: "Please see me. Josie." Then on second thought, I added, "Head Librarian" and underlined it.

Not an hour later, Wanda appeared at my office door, holding the note as if it were coated in acid. "Josie?"

I swiveled toward her and gestured to the armchair near me. "Please, have a seat." Thanks to Rodney's frequent naps in the chair, she'd have cat fur on her rear end. Pete the cat would approve.

Clearly suspicious, Wanda lowered herself on the chair. "I only have a minute. I have work to do."

I smiled. "That's what I wanted to talk with you about."

I felt a furry bump on my calf. Rodney. He had hidden under the desk. With my foot, I gently eased him out of view.

"Your job," I began, "is to keep Children's Literature tidy and to help people find the books they need."

"Is this about the lady yesterday? The one who got so mad when I gave her my opinion about a book?"

"You're entitled to your views, Wanda."

"Of course I am."

"But you're not entitled to make patrons feel uncomfortable. The children's room is set aside for kids to pull whatever books they want from the shelves. They should feel free to explore. Parents need to know they're not judged if they choose a story for their kids that happens to feature something you don't like. None of that can happen when you're openly questioning their choices." I kept my tone even and friendly and sensed the cheers from every shelf in Old Man Thurston's office.

Wanda stood so suddenly that her chair bumped against the low shelf behind her. However, her voice was deceptively nonchalant. I could see a thousand thoughts racing through her mind—thoughts she wouldn't tell me.

"I'm so glad we had this talk. I'd better get back to work."

"Just a moment," I said. "Does this have anything to do with Rodney? I noticed you seem uncomfortable when he's around."

She kept a hand on the doorknob. "I find it curious that a cat runs loose in a public institution."

That was neither a yes nor a no. "If he bothers you, I can keep him upstairs when you're here."

"I didn't say that. This is a bigger issue than Rodney."

Maybe Mona's foster charges bothered her, too? I was puzzled. "Tell me more."

Wanda's gaze skipped to the bookshelf, the window, and my desk before landing back on me. "It's simply that I want what's best for Wilfred."

"That's laudable. I'm glad we agree. What we may not agree on is what *best* means. While I'm librarian, *best* at the library means that mothers can choose books for their children without our commentary on their choices." I softened my voice. "You understand that, don't you, Wanda?"

As if agreeing, Rodney nudged my ankle with his silky nose.

A stiff smile spread across her face. It looked almost painful. "Perhaps it would be better if I didn't volunteer here."

"If that's how you feel about it, perhaps you're right," I said.

Wanda opened the door, then turned once more toward me. "Goodbye, Josie. You, too, Rodney."

Chapter Fourteen

On my lunch break, I called Lalena. "Do you have a second?" I asked.

"I have a tarot card reading for Dylan in ten minutes. Why?" she asked.

I pictured Lalena setting out the tarot cards on her linoleum-topped kitchen table. All through high school, Dylan had been our intern, and he'd charmed patrons in his vintage suits, culled from his dead grandfather's closet, and his regular references to Cary Grant films. Now he was preparing for college. I hadn't known he was into divination, but the movie *I'm No Angel*, with Mae West and Cary Grant, featured a fortune teller. That might have persuaded him to give it a try.

"It's about Ian," I said. "Have you heard from him?"

"No. What do you know?" she asked quickly.

"I have an idea, that's all. Can you call me when you're finished with Dylan?" I didn't want to say anything that could further upset, or mistakenly hearten, her until I had better information.

An hour later, instead of calling, Lalena turned up at the library in person. "What did you want to tell me about Ian?" she asked, breathless from hurrying up the hill.

I was in the conservatory, cleaning up after a midday meeting of the crochet club, an offshoot of the knitting club formed when a faction of knitters disagreed about the superiority of knitting over crochet, an argument that had devolved into unflattering comments about one another's stitching abilities and yarn choices. In my two years in Wilfred, I'd seen the crochet club rise and fall three times as members fought and made up. Soon the knitting club would be whole again.

"Have a seat." I lifted a few snips of rose-colored wool from a chair. "You haven't heard from Ian at all, right? No missed calls? Nothing?"

Eyes wide, she shook her head. "No. I told you so."

Once again I remembered Ian's body on the atrium floor. Lalena caught me glancing toward the doorway to the atrium, and she followed my gaze, an eyebrow raised. I hoped what I'd seen hadn't been real, maybe a misplaced vision of what had happened to him. I turned to her.

"And you're certain he's gone, not that you've simply missed him somehow."

Despite her obvious pain, Lalena was losing patience with me. "He's gone. We'd never gone a day without talking, and now it's been almost a week. Besides that. . . ." As her words trailed off, she examined the floor.

I stooped to pick up a stray piece of yarn near where she stared. "Besides that, what?"

"I broke into his trailer."

I stood suddenly. "Say that again?"

"Don't get so high and mighty. You've broken into a few places."

Lalena was right, and she'd even helped me once. I'd only done it under life-or-death circumstances, however. I was beginning to wonder if Ian's disappearance counted. "He wasn't there." Buffy and Thor's surveillance had proven that much.

"I knew he wasn't there. I wanted to see if he'd left any sort of clue." Her voice caught. "The milk carton was on the counter, like you said. I put it away."

It was undoubtedly sour by now, but Lalena had probably wanted some way to feel she was doing something productive. "Could you tell if he'd packed a suitcase?"

"Not really. I don't even know if he owns a suitcase. His wheelchair wasn't there, of course, and his bed hadn't been slept in." She twisted her hands. "His coffee cup and cereal bowl were in the sink. It was like he dropped everything after breakfast and never came home."

Again, I urged Lalena to sit, and I took the chair next to hers. "Anything else?"

"He'd taken his medication with him," she said. "Because of his injury, he takes blood thinners."

Which prompted another thought. Whether it was helpful, I wasn't sure. "Do you know how he lost the use of his legs?"

"No. Why would that have anything to do with why he left?"

"I don't know. You have to admit he's secretive about it."

Her lips tightened. "It's none of our business."

"I'm sorry. Of course you're right. I—"

"Don't apologize. I've wondered, too. He won't talk about it."

The grandfather clock in Popular Fiction chimed. Soon some of the laborers from the nearby rose nursery would be coming in for instruction in English as a second language.

Time to float my theory. "He left at about the time the construction crew showed up at the Empress, right?"

"Yes."

"Have you seen Lise Bloom?"

"The lady with the freckles? The stranger?"

I nodded. I didn't know any way to soften my next question. "I can't figure out what she wants in Wilfred, but she's been wandering around for a few days now. What if she's someone from Ian's past, and he wants to avoid her?"

Lalena leaned forward, and her words came in a rush. "You mean, an old girlfriend?"

"I didn't want to bring it up, but we need to consider every angle. Do you know anything about his romantic history?"

"It would have been a really nasty breakup to make him leave town without a word," she said. "But to answer your question, no, I don't know about his past relationships." She looked at her fingers, then added in a quiet voice, "Do you think he was married and abandoned her?"

It sounded outrageous, but wasn't unheard of. Maybe he was shirking fatherhood or owed her money. Maybe he was simply ashamed and didn't want Lalena to know about her. Extreme, but possible. Ian had kept a lot about his life hidden. Plus, the timing fit.

"I don't know. It was a thought," I said.

Lalena stared, unseeing, toward the potted banana tree. Surprisingly, when she looked up again, it was with a happy glow. "If it's true, it's good news." At my puzzled expression, she added, "It means he's alive."

I hoped she was right. If only Sam and I were on better terms, I could ask him to look into Lise Bloom. Even without him, however, I could still nose around. As that thought settled into my brain, a book title wafted through the ether: *Think Again: The Power of Knowing What You Don't Know*. What did that mean?

"I'll see if I can get some answers," I promised. Maybe Lise Bloom would have them.

Chapter Fifteen

That night after work, I called the retreat center and, fortunately, didn't get Wanda on the phone. Lucky as that was, it meant I didn't know if Lise was in. Another call to the café confirmed that Lise's Kia was in the retreat center's parking lot, so she was still in Wilfred. I'd keep a lookout for her.

In the meantime, however, I could check out what was happening at the Empress. Once again, I wondered: could Ian have encountered someone he knew when the construction crew moved in? Perhaps someone who could broadcast something about his past that he didn't want known?

I made my way down the hill. Orson wouldn't have started his shift at the tavern yet, and maybe I could catch him. I stopped on the bridge over the Kirby River—more of a creek this time of year—to rest my palms on the cool stone balustrade and watch the water drowse past with tufts of cottonwood seeds here and there.

The parking lot at Darla's Café was already filling up with pickup trucks and cars full of families looking for an easy weeknight dinner. I walked past it, past Patty's This-N-That, its windows dark but the memory of Babe Hamilton lingering, and found Orson outside the Empress, surveying its progress.

He greeted me with a salute of his coffee mug. "Josie. How goes it? Isn't she lovely?"

We gazed at the Empress, looking, to me at least, more rundown than lovely. The cinema's vinyl siding had been ripped off, revealing peeling tar paper and the rotting planks of its original siding, along with the ghost of a painted ad for Packard cars. The building's few windows were open cavities. A mess of weather-aged shingles were piled toward the rear. Orson clearly saw the potential, not the current reality.

I got down to business. "Have you seen Ian lately?"

He shook his head. "Still gone, is he?"

Gone was one word for it, I thought, remembering the specter of his body in the library. "He can't be far. His van is still here. I wondered if he'd stopped by late at the tavern."

"Nope." Orson tipped his coffee mug all the way back, then examined its depths. "He's done a runner. Take my word for it—I've seen it before. Darla's second husband, for instance. Kirk, I believe his name was." Apparently having exhausted interest in his mug, he looked at me. "I don't know what we're going to do with all that milk."

Before marrying Montgomery, Darla had hooked up with a string of losers. Why any one of them would leave her, however, was beyond me. "Ian is better than that, I hope."

"Kirk thought the world owed him a golden throne and a kingdom to lord over. Spending his days fishing and drinking while Darla worked wasn't enough for him. I wonder where he ended up?"

While fascinating, Darla's romantic history wasn't why I'd sought Orson. "Ian disappeared at about the same time work started on the Empress. Could the two be connected?"

"Lalena doesn't have the cleanest history with fellows, you know. Always going after the ones who were too slippery to get caught. Although I did think it was different with Ian."

"Me, too. Which is why I wonder if someone on the crew scared him off."

Orson set his coffee mug on the bumper of a construction rig and cupped his chin in his hand to ponder my question. "You mean, did he see someone he'd rather not run into? He is a mysterious guy. Never would say how he ended up in a wheelchair. Roz once tried to get him liquored up to talk about his past, but he stuck to his milk and didn't give a thing. All I know is he's from Baltimore, and I only know that because he keeps an eye on the Orioles on the tavern's TV."

Aha, Baltimore. That fit. "You're sure? Maybe he likes the team for other reasons."

"You mean because it's named after a bird? That'd be Ruth's shtick. No, we talked about it. He's from Baltimore, all right."

"How about the construction crew? How did you find them?"

"I didn't advertise in Baltimore, if that's what you're getting at."

I gave Orson my best *as if* glance. "Seriously. Where did you find them?"

"Like everyone else, I took bids from construction companies. I liked this one out of Portland. Decent price, and the project manager really got my concept. 'The Empress Taproom.'" Orson let out a contented sigh. "The tavern's all well and good, but Wilfred is ready for a classy joint."

Construction workers could easily travel. It wasn't out of the question that one of them hailed from Baltimore. "You don't happen to have a list of the subcontractors, do you?" Maybe insurance would require it of him.

"Nope. You need to go to Tyrone Beaudrie for that." He parked his hands on his hips and looked up at the Empress, now more of a scraggly street urchin than royalty. "You know, I wouldn't be surprised if Tyrone is an East Coaster. I stirred him a martini the other night, and he asked for a vodka from New York." He shook his head. "I told him, we have plenty of fine liquor out here. People and their snobberies. Martini drinkers are the worst, if you ask me. I'd take an old-fashioned drinker over a martini drinker any night of the week. Then there are Negroni drinkers, like that new gal."

My ears perked. "New gal?"

"Kind of reminds me of you, but freckled. A sweet lady. I made her a Negroni the other night, and the first thing she did was pull it up to her nose and sniff it." He smiled with satisfaction. "She really appreciates crafts-manship in a cocktail. Said she could smell the Cynar I subbed for Campari."

"You must mean Lise Bloom."

"If that's the name of the gal staying at the retreat center, then it's her." He nodded slowly. "Funny, she was asking about you, too."

Me? "What did she want to know?"

He shrugged. "Nothing in particular. Told her you were a librarian."

Stranger and stranger. Could Lise Bloom be from Baltimore? This bore following up.

"If you're going to ask me if I've seen her since," Orson said, "the answer is no."

After talking with Orson, I walked the two blocks to the Wallingford Guest House to find Tyrone Beaudrie. Night was falling, and dusk clung to front yard trees. I glanced behind me, knowing this was the moment the few clouds in the sky would show orange and pink underbellies as the sun lowered on the horizon. Now that my magic was back in full force, Wilfred's beauty practically made me tipsy.

The Wallingford Guest House was in a renovated Queen Anne with a wide porch festooned with ginger-bread. The guest rooms were all on the second floor. Tonight the ground-floor rooms were warm with lamp-light through the lace sheers, but the upstairs rooms were dark. Tyrone wasn't there. I didn't even bother to mount the porch steps and ask for him.

I retraced my steps and headed for the café. Unless he had driven into Forest Grove or Portland, Tyrone would be at Darla's. There was nowhere else in town to go.

My one fear about approaching the café was that I'd run into Babe Hamilton. She would have to know I'd broken her spell. Would she try something else—something more dangerous? Or would she leave in defeat? The crows that had dogged me the past months had vanished, and I didn't sense a renewed dampening of my magic. However, I didn't want to drop my guard.

Buffy and Thor were at the café's entrance, stopping incoming customers. I placed a protective hand on my purse.

"Josie," Buffy said, turning a coy eye toward me as I approached. "Need fashion advice? I didn't want to say anything, but you dress kind of boring."

That was their line today? Fashion consultations? I looked from Thor's cape and eyepatch, now turned up, to Buffy's glitter-spangled tutu and lime-green T-shirt sporting a unicorn. My wardrobe tended to be a comfortable mix of jeans, cotton skirts, and practical shoes. Unicorns and capes wouldn't add much to my cachet as a librarian.

"No thanks," I told them. "But how would you like to earn a dollar each? It will take you two minutes."

"Doing what?" Buffy said.

"Just tell me if Babe Hamilton is anywhere inside."

"We can't go in the tavern," Thor said. "We're just kids, you know."

"That's okay. Check the patio and café."

After a shared glance, they took off, Buffy to the café

and Thor to the patio. They returned, breathless, holding out their palms. "No Babe," Buffy said.

"That will be two dollars each," Thor added.

"One dollar each," I corrected. I doled out the bills.

"Why do you care where Babe is?" Buffy asked. "She didn't come into the shop today."

"Never mind. Here comes your grandma."

Patty crossed the narrow highway that served as Wilfred's main street. "Kids, it's time for bed. Stop bothering Josie and get over here."

Buffy and Thor ran off to greet her, and I turned to the café. A quick survey of the café and patio not only confirmed that Babe Hamilton wasn't there; Tyrone Beaudrie wasn't, either. I went to the doorway connecting the café and tavern and let my vision adjust to the lowered light. There he was, at a booth along the far wall. I returned to the counter at the café and ordered a bowl of Cajun macaroni and cheese to be delivered to the tavern.

"Tyrone?" I hovered at the edge of his booth.

Tyrone Beaudrie was examining a wide set of blueprints. With only the illumination from a low-wattage bulb in the red-shaded lamp on the wall above us, they couldn't have been easy to read.

"Thanks, but I'm still working on this." Tyrone touched his nearly full pint of beer.

"I'm not the server. Josie Way, librarian. Remember? We talked a few days ago."

"Yes." He smiled, and charm replaced his tired expression. "Sorry. It's dark in here. It's a pleasure to see you. Please, have a seat."

I slid into the bench across from him, aware of a

freshly photocopied poster tacked above the low wall sconce. CONCERNED WILFREDIANS FOR A BETTER LIBRARY, the poster read. It invited people to attend a talk the next night at the retreat center to "address vital issues concerning our community library."

I cursed silently. Wanda was behind this. I was sure. I put a hand to my temple and rubbed it. Tyrone noticed my reaction.

"You don't know about this?" he asked, nodding at the poster.

"No. I. . . ." I didn't want to get into it. Wanda had something up her sleeve, and I had a feeling I wouldn't like it. "I'll deal with that later. I came to find you tonight because—"

"You hunted me down?"

I ignored his playful grin. "I have an odd question for you."

He rolled up the plans and tucked them beside him on the bench. "Odd as it might be, I'll entertain any question coming from you."

He was flirting. Again, he didn't tempt me, but again I appreciated the attention. "Not that."

"Then you want to know when the Empress Brewpub will be finished." He lifted his pint glass and returned it to the table. "Beer here isn't bad but could be improved. Not to mention the atmosphere. I don't want to sound like a snob," Tyrone added quickly, "but this town could use variety."

I couldn't help but laugh at his canny summary of Wilfred's entertainment options. "I won't argue with that. But, no, that wasn't my question."

Tyrone raised an eyebrow. A smile spread across his lips. "Gotcha. Let me buy you a drink."

"It's about your crew," I said. "Nothing else."

"Sure." He didn't believe me. He leaned back, his smile widening. "Ask away."

"Are any of them from Baltimore?"

His smile morphed to a frown. "What? Why do you ask?"

Just then, one of the Tohler girls—they seemed to rotate through the café as servers; when one went to college, another one stepped in, and they looked uncannily similar—slid a bowl and a napkin-wrapped bundle of silverware in front of me. "Mac and cheese."

"Thanks, Tanya," I said. Or was it Tallulah? "What's going on with these posters?"

"Darla okayed them. The new custodian at the retreat center asked her to put them up."

It was Wanda, all right. I returned my attention to Tyrone. "I wanted to talk to you about someone in Wilfred who's from Baltimore. He disappeared about the same time the construction crew arrived. His girlfriend is worried about him. We thought maybe he saw someone he knew, someone with the construction crew, and took off."

"Someone he had a beef with."

I shrugged. "Maybe. Why else would he leave?"

"People split town for lots of reasons. Could have owed money. Had a family emergency. Maybe he wasn't so happy with his girlfriend." His seductive smile returned. "Although if she's anything like you, that would be hard to believe."

I looked at my hands to hide my almost-certain blush. "I didn't see any sign of any of that."

"You wouldn't. That's the point." He gestured to my macaroni and cheese. "Don't wait on my accord. You'd better eat that before it gets cold." I picked up a fork, and he continued. "As it happens, I'm from Baltimore."

I put down my fork again. "You?"

He nodded. "I haven't seen anyone here I know from back home." He leaned forward. "Only a few I'd like to know better."

Baltimore. All the way here on the West Coast. What were the odds? "Did you know anyone named Ian Penclosa?"

He looked genuinely baffled. "Penclosa. I can honestly say no. You weren't, um, close to him, too, were you?"

"Friend of a friend." I couldn't help flirting back. This man was a snake charmer, only with women and not cobras. "Are all the men in Baltimore players like you?"

He laughed. "Maybe your missing friend is. Seriously, though, what does he look like?"

"Dark hair, a scar on his face. The first thing you might notice is he's in a wheelchair."

Tyrone might have looked startled for a moment, but I also might have been mistaken. Or maybe my description wasn't what he'd expected. Slowly, he shook his head. "No. Doesn't ring a bell."

I turned my attention to the food in front of me. Maybe I'd come up dry on information about Ian, but I'd scored a hit with dinner. Darla's mac and cheese was loaded with homemade andouille and just enough bell pepper to give it interest.

"I think I'll order one of those." He raised his hand, and Orson ambled over.

When Orson returned a few minutes later with Tyrone's dinner, Wanda stood behind him. She nodded toward the poster. "I'm sorry I wasn't able to talk to you about it first, but when Ruth told me the trustees' meeting was coming up, I didn't have enough time. Now that you know, I'd like to formally invite you to attend."

I forced a smile. "I'm glad to see you have so much interest in the library. Can you tell me what the meeting is about?"

"I have concerns." Whatever those concerns were, Wanda felt confident they'd override any of my objections. I saw it in her smug expression.

"Does it have to do with Rodney?" No one else complained about him running free in the library. If anything, he was a draw. The thought of having to keep him cooped up in my apartment broke my heart and would certainly break his.

"In a way, yes," she replied. "Can I count on you coming?"

I didn't have much choice—not if it involved the library. "Yes, I'll be there."

"Good. Good evening." With a flamenco-adjacent sashay in her walk, she left the tavern.

Tyrone jerked a thumb toward the door, still swinging, to the café. "You have trouble with her?"

I toyed with my dinner. "I'm not sure yet. She's stirring things up, and I'm wary."

"She works for you?"

"She's a volunteer. At least, she was until this afternoon. We mutually agreed she wasn't a good fit," I said.

He nodded knowingly. "Got it. You did well to nip this in the bud. Give someone like her a few inches, and she'll make a grab for it. I've had a lot of experience with this sort of thing."

"Thank you. I'd thought that by talking to her about how she interacted with patrons that I'd settled the matter. Instead, I'd instigated a town meeting."

"The library is your world, remember. She's just a visitor."

The rest of the evening passed quickly. Tyrone was charming dinner company, and it felt good to have a man's attention to distract me from my failed relationship with Sam. We picked right up from our earlier conversation. He asked more about Ian and about life in Wilfred, and I found myself opening up to him. In turn, I asked him about the challenges of running a construction job, and he regaled me with stories of absent plumbers, "creative" architects, and mouthy drywallers. He said he was almost certain most of his crew was local, but he'd give me a list of subcontractors to see if I could track any of them back to Baltimore.

All this time, I remembered his employee's warning about him. "I hope you don't think this is too forward, but earlier this week I heard you arguing with someone in your crew."

Tyrone pushed his empty bowl to the side. "Cliff." He shook his head. "I . . . it's . . . we go way back. This is the last job I'll work with him. I can't take his behavior any longer." He looked me straight in my eyes. "Take my advice and stay away from him."

"Funny," I said, my pulse leaping a notch. "That's what he told me about you."

Tyrone's expression froze, and a muscle twitched in his jaw. For a moment, I wondered if he was angry. Then he laughed. "He would say that. It might be that I've been successful with the ladies a few times when he's struck out."

When we left the tavern, Tyrone opening the door for me, night had fallen. The door closed, shutting off the bar's country-western music and chatter. Tyrone tucked a hand in the small of my back.

I turned to him to tell him, "Hands off, buddy," and heard "Hello, Josie" from the parking lot.

There was no mistaking that voice. It was Sam, showing a faint glimmer of a smile. In other words, he wasn't happy. Despite this, angels might have been singing at my elation at seeing him.

I didn't have time to reply before he disappeared into the café.

Chapter Sixteen

At last, it was my day off. Tyrone Beaudrie had promised to have a list of his crews ready for me by noon. Until then, there wasn't much I could do, except ponder the meager information I had about Ian's disappearance and look for Lise. That, and fret about tonight's meeting about the library.

I set off toward the retreat center, taking the long way through town so I could formulate an approach if I was unlucky enough to run into Wanda. It was a fine morning, and the breeze off the river was refreshingly cool. Rodney scampered ahead as I wandered down the hill and into town.

Walking was a good time to think, and I had a lot to think about. The distance between Sam and me continued to eat at me. He wouldn't answer my texts, and last night he wouldn't even make eye contact. I could show up at his house and demand an explanation for why he so suddenly lost interest, but I knew the answer. Once I'd opened up about being a witch, he wanted no part of me. This realization stung. If he wasn't a big enough man to talk to me about it, I needed to let him go. Yet I couldn't.

Babe Hamilton—Aunt Beata—also haunted my thoughts. As if reading my mind, Rodney stopped nosing a Douglas fir and examined me. My great aunt, here in Wilfred. Here and deliberately hampering my magic. How had she found me? Buffy and Thor said she hadn't shown up at the This-N-That yesterday. I felt strong in my power again but feared she was planning another assault.

Then there was this mysterious meeting tonight about library "issues." Why hadn't Wanda talked to me before going public? Her growing friendship with Ruth Littlewood concerned me, too. Ruth was a formidable opponent. If they both took a position I didn't like, such as banning Rodney from the library, I'd face a tough battle. Libraries should be supportive, nurturing spaces, not hotbeds of controversy. As this thought passed through my mind, I saw another poster outside the P.O. Grocery advertising tonight's meeting.

My wandering led me to the lot behind the church cemetery, where Lyndon and Roz's house was being built. Just last spring, the lot was a stretch of mud with a dilapidated outhouse covered in blackberry vines— and hosting human bones. All evidence of crime was now replaced with a fresh foundation and the exterior shell of a bungalow-style house. Duke and Desmond were setting a window at the house's rear.

"Hello, Josie," Lyndon said. He was kneeling next to a potted tree peony. "Looking good, hey?"

"You'll have everything closed up well before the

rain starts," I said. "Have you seen Lise Bloom, the woman staying at the retreat center?"

"Nope," Lyndon said.

Roz leaned out the window opening nearby. "Look," she said. "My office."

Rodney jumped to the window ledge. I leaned near him to peer inside at framed-in walls and a concrete floor. It was easy to imagine Roz's desk against the window and bookshelves along the walls.

"Lyndon is planting a peony tree so I have something to inspire me while I write." She cast a dreamy glance toward him. Her gaze drifted to Rodney, and her expression snapped to seriousness. "Have you seen the notices around town? About the library meeting?"

"I ran into Wanda last night. I'm not worried about it," I said with more conviction than I felt.

"I wouldn't be so cavalier." Roz crossed her arms and leaned on a wall stud. "I heard her at the café last night. People are listening to her."

"Do you know what she's so worked up about?"

"Cats. She says they're a plague on society."

Rodney backed up and jumped off the window ledge. He wanted no part of this conversation.

"That's crazy talk. I think she's scared of them. She wouldn't tell me about her agenda for the meeting, but my guess is she wants to ban Rodney from the library."

"It's worse than that. She says cats are predators and terrorize birds."

"Ruth Littlewood would be sympathetic," I said. That explained their secret tête-à-têtes.

"Ruth's not the only bird watcher in town. Marcus

Dortmunder, besides having two budgies, has always hated cats, ever since Snowball—that was before your time—got in through his kitchen window and stole a pork chop he'd broiled for his and Evelyn's anniversary dinner. Plus, Katie Linn heard a story about cats smothering babies in their cradles. She said her husband's sister's mother-in-law's neighbor found her Maine coon in the baby's crib. The baby was okay, but who knows what might have happened? Those are big cats." Roz snapped open her fan and batted it in the air. At this point, the fan was less about hot flashes and more a tool to emphasize her glass-half-empty opinions. "I wouldn't dismiss Wanda. She's surprisingly convincing when she's worked up."

"Do you know anything about her? Why is she in Wilfred, anyway?" I asked.

"She's a birdwatcher, like Ruth. Obsessed with hawks," Duke said. I hadn't known he was listening. "Flamenco dancer, too. Plus an ace kickboxer. She needed to get away from a relationship gone bad, so when I saw the opening at the retreat center, I thought of her right away."

"I saw her dancing at the retreat center," I said. If Wilfred had taught me anything, it was a lesson all librarians should know: never judge a book by its cover.

"Clever, Wanda is," Duke said. "Ever since she was a kid. She made tap shoes out of a pair of oxfords by driving nails into their heels. Bam, bam!" He mimicked thrashing a hammer into a shoe. The violence of his demonstration made me jump.

Roz pointed a finger at Duke. "See? Don't underestimate her."

"What has she got against cats?" I asked Duke. "She seems afraid of Rodney."

He leaned his level against the house. Desmond stepped forward to listen. "Oh no, it's not fear. She detests 'em."

"I figured that out," I said. "What I want to know is, why?"

"It didn't used to be that way," Duke said. He shifted foot to foot in a way that signaled he was settling in for a story.

"Tell me more," I said.

"She used to have a cat, a tabby named Tabby. Tabitha, for real." He looked up to make sure I understood.

"Tabby the tabby cat. Got it," I said.

"Wanda loved that cat. The cat slept in her bed, followed her everywhere."

"What happened?" I guessed that the cat ran away—or worse.

"Tabby moved out. My brother Arthur got a dog, and Tabby wouldn't stand for it. She moved in with the neighbors, a sweet old couple who fed her chicken livers."

"Cats do that sometimes," Desmond noted.

It would break my heart if Rodney ever got it into his head to move. "That's why she hates cats."

"Nope," Duke said. "She was deathly allergic, so it wasn't a big loss."

"Cut to the chase, Duke," Roz said.

"Wanda, see, got engaged to a veterinarian. Not long ago, just after she left the army. She met him flamenco dancing."

Wanda in the army? Somehow it fit. "Go on."

"He brought cat hair and dander home every day. She was miserable. Her eyes swelled up, she talked funny because she was congested, and she had terrible headaches. She told him he had to stop treating cats, just stick to dogs, but he refused. They canceled the wedding the morning of the ceremony."

"You're kidding," Roz said.

"That's awful," I said.

"Not so awful," Duke said. "I never liked the guy. If you ask me, he was looking for a reason to dump Wanda, and the cat bit was his excuse."

"But to leave her like that, with the dress in the closet and the invitations sent and accepted?" Roz said. "No wonder she left town."

"Wanda begged him to change his mind. She got allergy shots and everything, but he wouldn't budge. Not six months later, he married the owner of four longhaired Persians. From then on, she's loathed cats."

Roz pushed back from the open space that would soon be her office window. "Kickboxing, Josie. Just saying. You'd better take her seriously."

Roz's warning ringing in my ears, I wandered past the Wallingford Guest House and waved at the owner's daughter, who was twirling two batons in their front yard.

"Hi, Ellie. Have you seen the lady staying at the retreat center?"

She spun and caught both batons before responding. "Nope."

From there I passed to Wilfred's main drag and cast an eye toward the This-N-That. It wasn't yet open, so I didn't need to fear Babe Hamilton's presence.

The café's parking lot was packed, and the café would be full of families loading up on breakfasts of Darla's waffles, omelets, and famous shrimp and grits. The patio was busy, too, and I gave it a wide berth when I saw Wanda at a table near its edge, surrounded by a group in noisy conversation. No Lise.

With Wanda occupied, I could safely look for Lise at the retreat center. Maybe she'd returned. I took a left toward the entrance to the Magnolia Rolling Estates just beyond the café to use as a shortcut through the meadow. Ian's trailer lacked signs of life. The windows were dark, and his van hadn't moved. Poor Lalena. I knew her anguish.

Similarly, the curtains were drawn at Babe's trailer. I felt a twinge of foreboding with no logical reason behind it. Babe's spell was broken. I was safe. Or was I? Another thought crossed my mind: Had I ever seen both Babe and Lise in the same place?

The meadow was still damp with morning dew, but the sun on my shoulders told me it wouldn't be for long. Rodney ran ahead of me and pounced on something I couldn't see before a quick bout of zoomies in the buttercups.

I took the path over the levee dividing the river from the millpond and came out near the stone patio in front of the retreat center. Lise's car was in the lot. The center's lobby door was unlocked, so I entered its main room, taking in the building's cathedral ceiling and shoulder-height fireplace.

"Lise?" I called out. No response.

I poked my head into the kitchen and adjoining dining room, and those were empty, too. Well, I'd tried to find her. From the retreat center, I could return to the library along the path through the woods by the river.

I had made it as far as the retreat center's front door when a voice called for me from the upstairs landing. I looked up to see Lise staring down. A strange energy passed between us. I couldn't explain it, except to say it felt like an electrical shimmer.

"Josie?" Lise said. "I was just leaving to look for you."

I caught my breath. "I was looking for you, too."

"Let's go for a walk. There's a trail through the woods I've been wanting to explore." Lise was dressed for it—jeans and a cotton blouse—only they were vintage high-waisted denim capris and a men's shirt knotted at the waist. She looked as if she'd walked off the set of a 1950s movie set in the Maine woods.

We walked toward the trail that led along the Kirby River to the library and Big House. It had once been the graveled road Old Man Thurston used to drive to the timber mill where the retreat center now stood. Over the years, the road had grown over, and now only a footpath remained.

As soon as we entered the forest's canopy, the temperature dropped, and I slipped off my sunglasses. The air smelled moist and green. Here, birds, instead of chirping on the meadow floor, flitted high in the branches of conifers. By habit now, I listened for the cawing of crows, but heard nothing.

"It's so nice here," Lise said. "It smells like heaven—moss, pine, and rising heat."

A whisper of cinnamon, lavender, and rose settled around Lise like an aura. "Speaking of, you smell good, too. What is it?"

"You like it? It's an old perfume called Danger. It hasn't been made in decades. I got it at an estate sale."

As Lise talked, I found myself examining her for hints of Beata, but other than an apparent penchant for estate sales, I didn't see a connection. That said, I sensed something otherworldly about her. I reminded myself that Beata's glamour could make me see whatever she intended.

"You wanted to talk to me?" I asked. I was beginning to suspect I knew why she was in Wilfred, and it had to do with Ian. She had probably uncovered my friendship with Lalena and wanted to ask about him.

Lise stepped forward, into a shaft of light through the trees. It illuminated the red in her chestnut hair—red hair like mine. She didn't respond at first. I waited.

"I was wrong when I told you I didn't know why I was here. I'm looking for something. Someone, maybe."

I nodded. Just what I'd thought. "You're from Baltimore."

She looked at me oddly. "I live in Astoria. We talked about it."

"I mean, before you moved to Astoria. Do you know Ian Penclosa?"

"Who?" When I didn't respond—why was she here, then, if not for Ian?—Lise tipped up her chin to examine the treetops. Rodney brushed against the pants of her jeans, and when she glanced down, he skittered into the ferns.

"Do you believe in magic?" she asked.

The question caught me off guard. "What? Why?"

Something in her relaxed. "You didn't say *no*."

"You're right," I replied, but declined to explain further. "What does that have to do with why you're here?"

"I met Leo. He told me about you." As she spoke, she watched me carefully to gauge my reaction.

"You know Leo?" Leo, the man I'd met the year before, the man researching the documentary about folk magic. What had he said to Lise Bloom? "How is he these days?"

"He said he thinks you're a witch."

My breath stuck in my throat. I fought to keep a level expression. "He's been spending too much time reading about old spells. If I was a witch"—here, I forced a laugh—"what's it to you? Witch hunting went out centuries ago."

She looked away. "It's nothing. I don't know what I was thinking."

Yet it clearly was something to her; otherwise, why would she find it so urgent to ask me about it? I remembered the witch-centered novels she borrowed at the retreat center. "You came to Wilfred because you thought I was a witch and wanted to check me out? You're not here because of Ian?"

She looked strangely disappointed. "I don't know who Ian is."

He might have changed his name when he came to Oregon. "The used book seller in Patty's This-N-That. Dark hair, a scar right here." I patted my right cheek.

"Nope." She had lost interest in me since I hadn't claimed my magic. She pointed off the trail. "Did you see that clearing in the woods? Someone made a fire."

The witch's circle was a solid ten-minute walk from the trail, which meant she must have been wandering in the woods. A casual hiker wouldn't have found it. If I hadn't known it was there, I wouldn't have found it, either. "You went into the woods?"

"I smelled smoke." She turned toward the barely visible trail through the underbrush. "A dead fire, that is."

She must have an incredible nose. I adopted a dismissive tone. "Campers, likely. Or kids from the high school."

"I see."

We both knew how unlikely it was that campers or teenagers would find their way to this obscure part of the forest. I still wondered how Lise had found it. I sure couldn't smell anything. Had she really come all the way to Wilfred to see if I was a witch? Or was she a witch herself—in short, was she Aunt Beata?

"I'll be moving along, then," Lise said. "I'll tell Leo you said hi."

"A witch," I replied. "As if."

Chapter Seventeen

As I walked home, I pondered what Lise had told me. Leo had labeled me a witch. That, in itself, didn't concern me. Thanks to his research, Leo was steeped in folk magic, and people probably figured he saw witches everywhere. Besides, his definition of *witch* was fluid and applied to regular people who cast spells as well as those rumored to have magical abilities. History interested him. Folk tradition. I didn't even know if he believed in magic.

Why had she brought it up at all? Unless she had magic, too. I'd felt a gut-level connection with Lise, but I couldn't tell if I should trust it or stay far away.

Rodney emerged from the brush to follow me along the trail. After a dozen yards or so, he dashed into the bushes again. A few steps later, I saw why. One of the workers from the Empress's renovation was ambling toward me. He lifted his baseball cap and raked a hand through dirty hair.

For a split second I wondered if I should be worried

by his furtive glances to the side. Here, if I screamed, no one would hear me. The nearest building was the library, and that I knew to be empty.

Then the construction worker smiled, and my fear dropped away. I recognized him as Cliff, the man arguing with Tyrone earlier in the week, the one who lived in his van. No wonder Cliff was out stretching his legs on the trail, although I would have thought he'd be at work.

There was no way we could pass each other without a greeting.

"Hello," I said. "I'm surprised to see you. I didn't think many people knew about this trail."

"Why not? It seemed like a good afternoon for a walk."

I raised an eyebrow at his defensive tone. "Obviously, I agree." Tyrone had said that he and Cliff went "way back." Did that include way back to Baltimore?

Cliff looked to the right and left. "Nice day."

Not much I could say to that. "How do you like Wilfred?"

"It's all right, I guess." He stepped forward. "I heard you and Tyrone were talking at the tavern."

Cliff may have warned me off Tyrone, but that didn't mean I had to follow his every command. Besides, I barely knew the man. I braced myself. "That's right. You told me to stay away from him."

"I warned you. Don't believe anything he says." Cliff turned to leave.

"Just a moment, please. What, specifically, has Tyrone done that makes him so dangerous?"

Cliff opened his mouth, then closed it and nodded. "I've already said too much. I'll be moving on."

"One more thing," I said, before he'd taken more than a few steps. "Are you from Baltimore?"

"Am I what?"

"Baltimore." I quickly searched for the right way to say it. "I know someone in Wilfred originally from Baltimore, and he thought he recognized an old friend in the crew at the Empress." Only a slight fib.

He looked at me with curiosity. "What's your friend's name?"

"Ian Penclosa," I said.

Cliff's expression cleared. "Never heard of him."

"It's probably nothing," I said. "So many new people in town." New subject. "Are you local?" I knew the answer, but it seemed the polite thing to ask.

He seemed to accept my explanation and let it go. "No. I'm camping in my van. I like the lifestyle." He smiled that vulnerable smile again. "In the construction business, framers are known as hard workers and hard partiers. I can't say they're wrong. I like to travel, see nice places like this." He took in the landscape—the fir trees, rich smell of pine needles and loam, the Delft blue sky. A song sparrow trilled in the background.

Once again, he turned to leave. We continued on our ways—me to the library, and Cliff, presumably, toward the retreat center and millpond.

I couldn't say I was getting closer to answers about Ian, but at least I'd eliminated Lise as a suspect. I also received a doubled-down warning against Tyrone. That is, if I could believe either one of them.

* * *

I was used to Lalena coming to the library for regular baths in the old mansion's mammoth clawfoot tub, but it was rare for me to visit her at home. Tonight she'd invited me to dinner. Both of us were in love with men who were MIA, and both of us felt it deeply. I suspected tonight might end up as a meeting of the Lonely Hearts Club. I wished I had more hope to offer her about Ian, but at least I could proffer one bit of news.

It was early evening when I made my way to the Magnolia Rolling Estates. I kept an eye on Babe Hamilton's trailer, just behind Lalena's. The curtains were drawn, and her car was gone. My magic still felt free and full, and books talked to me from the homes I passed—from a farming magazine in one home, hens clucking and a droned list of planting dates; from another home, a historical romance's orchestral waltz.

Through Lalena's screen door, I waved the bottle of pinot gris I'd brought.

Lalena, wearing a vintage chemise likely from Babe's stall at the This-N-That, answered the door. Her chemise would be perfectly safe since Babe—or should I call her Beata?—hadn't charmed it.

"We'd better not drink all of that," she said, "not if you're going to the meeting at the retreat center tonight."

With that, Rodney let out a mournful meow. I sighed. "Maybe I should have brought two bottles. You're coming, too, aren't you?"

"I can't. I have a communication at seven with Maggie Foster's grandmother. Maggie can't find her photo album anywhere and thinks her nana knows where it is."

Nana Foster had passed away last winter. She'd been known for her prowess at scrapbooking and likely had squirreled away a dozen albums.

"What's for dinner?" I asked. I didn't smell anything cooking, and the kitchen counters were bare.

"Hors d'oeuvres." Lalena opened the refrigerator. "Bean dip, pickle-flavored potato chips, crackers, cheese puffs, hickory smoked almonds, and malted milk balls." She turned to me. "Is that okay? It's too hot to cook."

I made a mental note to get out the antacids. "Sounds great."

"Let's eat outside. The heat has brought out a second flush of roses."

Normally I'd jump at the chance to sit in a lawn chair in the crazy quilt of roses, dahlias, and zinnias outside. When Lalena had inherited the trailer from her aunt, its yard had been an expanse of white rock. Slowly, Lalena had replaced the rock with fresh soil and plants, and now her yard matched her character: messy, lovely, and slightly eccentric.

Today, however, I was on the alert for Babe Hamilton. "Outside would be nice." As if I'd only just thought of it, I added, "Have you seen Babe lately?"

The cork gave a hollow *pop* as Lalena opened the bottle of wine. "Didn't you hear the news?"

"Hear what?"

"She's giving up her booth and leaving Wilfred. It was all really sudden. In fact, she might already be gone." She pushed aside the kitchen window's ruffled curtain. "Her car's not in the drive."

She'd left town? It couldn't be this easy. My magic

was truly powerful. I'd vanquished a witch. "I wonder why she left?"

Lalena shrugged. "Family emergency? Beats me."

When we'd settled outside, I sprang my news. "I might have a lead on Ian."

Lalena paused, malted milk ball in hand. "What?"

"Orson says Ian is from Baltimore. They've talked about it when Ian was watching baseball at the bar."

"Baltimore. Really?" Lalena's focus softened, as if she were picturing Ian as a kid among the row houses.

I nodded. "The construction manager at the Empress is from Baltimore, too. I wonder if Ian saw him—Tyrone Beaudrie is his name—and fled? They might have a past."

Lalena stared thoughtfully into the distance. "Tyrone. Ian never mentioned him. Of course, he never mentioned Baltimore, either. Tyrone is the snappy dresser, right?"

"Shined shoes, ironed button-down, that's him. I asked him if he knew Ian, but the name didn't ring any bells."

"If I'd brought up Baltimore to Ian, I bet he would have switched the conversation to Edgar Allan Poe." She drew her attention back to me. "What would scare him so much that he'd leave town without telling me?"

"I wish I knew." I pushed the pickle-flavored chips toward her. "It's the not-knowing that's the worst, isn't it?"

Sadly, I spoke from experience. Sam had cut me out of his life as if I'd never existed. If anyone had asked me a month ago if he'd ever do anything like this—refuse to even give me a reason for utterly ghosting me—I'd have insisted they were wrong. That it wasn't like him to behave that way. Sam had always acted with integrity. Once he returned all the way to the P.O. Grocery during a downpour to refund a quarter to the cashier who'd accidentally given him too much change.

But I was the wrong one. I'd revealed who I truly was, a witch, and therefore ceased to exist for him. That he wouldn't face me to explain hurt even more.

"Why does it always end like this?" Lalena asked. I'd never heard this kind of pain in her voice. "Always."

"Surely you've had good relationships, and you will again," I said.

"No."

"But," I said, "men love you. And you love them." Lalena had a reputation for falling for bad boys. Ian, although mysterious, had seemed like something new. Unless he wasn't.

"So what if men are interested in me?" She clasped her hands in her lap. "Sure, they're intrigued, and, sure, I know how to engage a guy looking for a diversion, but that doesn't mean I can keep a relationship going more than a few months. The thing is. . . ."

"What, Lalena?"

"The thing is, as I told you, I was sure it was different this time."

I understood. I had thought it was different for me, too. I had felt so at ease with Sam. Not that he was perfect, but I loved his quirks and felt confident he loved mine. Still, I asked, "How?"

She let out a sigh more eloquent than words. "It was so easy to talk with him. I felt I could be myself, and we had so much fun together." The look on her face broke my heart. "We did dumb stuff together, like pretend we were part of a reality TV show. We laughed so hard. You should see his Donald Duck impersonation."

I felt as if my grandmother's words were leaving my lips. "Your grief is proof of your love."

Lalena looked at me like I'd grown another head. "Where did that come from?"

"I'm right, aren't I?" I said. "You felt something special with Ian. The flip side of that feeling—of letting yourself be known so deeply—is the pain that comes with its loss."

In saying these words, I knew they were true. Even if Sam never looked my way again, I didn't regret my time with him. It had ended too soon, but it had been worth it.

A crow cawed from somewhere nearby, and I jolted to upright in my chair before relaxing again. *Babe was gone, and crows did exist outside of her*, I reminded myself.

"What?" Lalena said.

"Nothing." Then, seeing a few people walk down the trailer park's central lane followed by another clump of Wilfredians, I said, "Do you usually get this much traffic in the evening?"

"It's people on their way to Wanda's meeting." She cleared our plates from the table. "Don't you think you'd better go?"

Chapter Eighteen

The retreat center glowed against the darkening evening. Its doors were open, and Wilfredians spilled onto the stone patio. I didn't see Lise Bloom. If she was smart, she was somewhere peaceful, maybe at the café, relaxing over a bowl of gumbo.

I was among the last to arrive. I left the chirps of crickets in the meadow and edged into the retreat center's main room. Rows of metal folding chairs were full of neighbors, with Ruth Littlewood in front. Despite the fan whirling in the cathedral ceiling, it was stuffy.

Wanda stood at a podium flanked with posters on easels reading The Feline Myth: Save Future Generations. Each poster was illustrated with a beady-eyed black cat with hackles raised. I ignored the resemblance to Rodney. When we'd left Lalena's trailer, he'd trotted toward home. Hopefully he was holed up safely in my apartment by now.

"Thank you, everyone, for coming," Wanda said. Her voice boomed above the chattering audience. We quieted. "I'm gratified to see so many concerned citizens here."

I couldn't believe Wanda had orchestrated an entire evening just to raise public support to evict Rodney from the library. Also surprising was how many people had shown up. Wilfredians always did enjoy a good spectacle.

Wanda ostentatiously snapped a sheaf of notes. "Does everyone have a seat?"

I ducked toward the room's rear.

"Let's get started." She scanned the crowd, leaving a pause for drama. "Yes, many of you are concerned. However, I have no doubt many others are here because you believe my cause is ridiculous. You're here to see me fail. I assure you, you are wrong. Give me half an hour, and I will change your mind."

Wanda had a convincing way about her. I scrapped my earlier thought that she should be an actor. Why she'd gone into the custodial business instead of going to law school, I had no idea. Which didn't mean I would buy any part of her argument. No matter what, Rodney stayed. I could shuffle him off when patrons who were allergic or afraid visited, but he was a library fixture, and I felt sure most of the rest of the town agreed.

"I'll begin with the bottom line," Wanda said. "The future. Educating and strengthening future generations. I'm certain we agree on the importance of that. To that end, we must show a united front at the library trustees' meeting the day after tomorrow."

What did banning Rodney have to do with future generations? I sat straighter.

"Cats," Wanda said, "are misunderstood." She paused to let us take that in. "We see them as loving creatures who want nothing more than to purr and sit in our laps. This is a mistake."

Thinking of Rodney, I had to admit she was right. Although he did purr and enjoyed lap time, he had a mind of his own.

Wanda continued. "Cats were never meant to be domesticated. They are not the purring, fluffy creatures portrayed in the media. They are killing machines." She raised a palm to silence the murmurs in the audience. "You see cats as harmless, am I right? You envision them snuggling in a basket by the fire or sleeping gently at the foot of your bed.

"These are lies fed to us by the pro-cat demographic. As I said, cats are predators designed to kill other creatures. Their teeth can strip flesh from a carcass faster than you can say 'Jack the Ripper.'" She leaned forward, eyes narrowing. "How many sofas and upholstered chairs have been lost to their needle-sharp claws?"

Forget attorney. Wanda should have been a preacher.

Mona stood. "What about humans? Cats don't shoot innocent bystanders. They can't cheat on spouses and swindle people. Cats don't insult people behind their backs or burn down houses for the fun of it. Why pick on cats?"

Wanda remained calm. If anything, her smile widened. "The difference is that we can't avoid humans. Cats, on the other hand, are entirely avoidable."

Here it came, Wanda's petition to ban Rodney. I braced myself.

Wanda set down her notes. "This is why I propose removing from the library all children's books featuring cats."

What? This was what this meeting was about? I hadn't meant to say anything, but the words escaped me anyway. "You've got to be out of your mind." I didn't care how many cat-loving, flamenco-dancing veterinarians had left her at the altar. She was demented to think we should remove books just because cats were in them.

From above Wanda, through the railing on the second floor's open hall, I caught a flash of a black furry tail. *Uh-oh.*

"I don't even want to go into detail about cats who"— she lifted her nose as if confronted by a laundry basket heaped with the high school football team's dirty socks— "who smother babies in their cribs."

"There's no proof of—" started someone several rows ahead of me.

"Then where did these stories come from?" Wanda said. "We've all heard them, haven't we? As the saying goes, where there's smoke, there's fire." Not waiting for confirmation, she continued. "Romanticizing cats through books portraying them as innocent, wide-eyed creatures who do nothing but snuggle is worse than irresponsible. It's deadly." She returned to her notes. "The Wilfred library houses seventy-two children's books with cats as major characters."

So that's what she and Ruth Littlewood had been doing. Cataloguing children's books.

"Each of these stories," Wanda continued, "is another instrument of pro-cat propaganda."

Mrs. Wallingford stood. "Where's the research showing that letting children read stories with cats in them hurts society?"

Hearing these words out loud drove home how absurd Wanda's argument was. After a glance at the upstairs railing to make sure Rodney wasn't up to any tricks, I relaxed in my chair.

"Do you really need research when common sense tells you everything you need to know?" Wanda replied.

"Birds," came a firm voice from the front row. Ruth Littlewood. "Let's not forget about the damage cats do to birds. There's plenty of research behind that."

Duke stood abruptly, his chair screeching against the floor. I held my breath. Duke could come out anywhere on this issue, and however he settled, he was stubborn. And he was a library trustee. "I don't hold with removing books. I believe in freedom of speech. The First Amendment, am I right?"

"Get this straight," Wanda said. When I looked from one pugnacious set of jaw to the other, I could clearly see Wanda and Duke's family resemblance. "I agree with you. I'm not advocating getting rid of the books altogether. I simply want them removed from sight."

"Why not just limit access to them? Why take them away completely?" a woman to my right asked.

A moving bit of yellow caught my eye from the banister above Wanda. What was it? It looked like it was on wheels. Slowly, it jerked a few inches at a time. I didn't, however, see Rodney. That didn't mean he didn't have something up his furry paw. *Don't make trouble*, I willed him.

"Simply requiring parental permission to check out a book is not enough," Wanda replied. "What if you—rightly, I might add—forbid your daughter to read a certain book, but she hears about it from her friend at school who didn't have such protection? This little girl might grow up believing cats solve crimes, or wear hats and gloves, or want nothing more than to charm little kids. The culture spreading lies about these deadly and destructive animals has already spread too far. Let me reemphasize: our taxes go to support the library. Public money should not be spent on spreading damaging misinformation."

Wanda had gone too far. Besides, she hadn't been in town long enough to contribute a penny to the library's budget. I would not hear another word. I stood. "Say you succeed at getting the library's trustees to vote to pull all children's books that have cats in them. Then what? Where does it stop?" I turned to Sheri. "Sheri rides her bike everywhere."

She raised a hand. "Leave me out of this, Josie."

"Just a minute. This is important. Say Sheri, concerned about the environment, decides Wilfred's children should not be exposed to polluting vehicles. She might want all kids' books with cars and trucks in them to be pulled from the shelves."

Wanda looked at me in confusion. "Is this a joke?"

Mona shot up from her seat. "Talk about a joke. Cats have been vital, helpful members of society for millennia. The Egyptians revered them. Cats reduce disease by killing vermin. They provide loving company to the lonely. They're beautiful, wonderful creatures."

"Wonderful? Beautiful?" She made a noise that was

a cross between a sneer and a raspberry. "They're hateful, dangerous, vicious beasts. Nonsense. You wouldn't want kids to read about making bombs, would you? As if it's a joy?"

A creak and thump sounded from directly above Wanda. The moving yellow object was the retreat center's wheeled mop bucket. I was horrified but couldn't tear my eyes away. *Rodney!* I shouted silently, just as a rush of pine-cleanser-scented water poured from the banister above Wanda. The audience gasped, and people in the front row stood to shake drops of water from their laps and shoulders.

Wanda snorted and wiped her eyes. She was drenched from her head to her knees. She turned her head in time to glimpse black fur scampering away from the upturned mop bucket. I could practically hear Rodney snicker.

Her face purple with rage, Wanda forced words through her teeth. "Saturday night. The library trustees' meeting. I count on seeing you there."

Chapter Nineteen

I'd been the first person out the door of Wanda's meeting and wasted no time getting back to the library. I planned to turn off the ringer on my phone and pretend I wasn't home until the furor over Rodney's antics wore off.

I arrived, breathless, to find a note on the library's kitchen door, folded and crammed into the jamb. As I pulled it out and smoothed it, my first thought was that it was some anti-cat scribe. But no, it was from Tyrone Beaudrie. He didn't have my phone number and couldn't have texted.

I learned something about Ian, the note read. *Come see me when you get this.*

I looked at my phone. It was nearly nine o'clock, and the night was as black as Rodney's belly. Too late to see him? His note sounded urgent.

I turned around and headed back down the hill toward the Wallingford Guest House. I could at least see if his light was on.

Wilfred's streets were rapidly quieting. People who'd attended Wanda's meeting were dispersing to their homes and boosting open windows to the cool night air. Inside they would lay out coffee cups for the morning and kiss children good night. The few trucks in the café's parking lot showed that the tavern had its usual handful of late-night customers. Orson—or his Tohler replacement—would soon be gently easing them toward the door.

A light was on in the Wallingford Guest House, but it was downstairs. Perhaps Tyrone waited for me in the house's ground floor library. I mounted the steps to the wraparound porch. A figure moved behind the library's sheer curtains. I rapped on the window.

The figure—a woman—came to the door. It was Mrs. Wallingford. "Josie? Can I help you?"

"Tyrone asked me to stop by. Is he here?" I patted my pocket to show her the note, but it wasn't there. I could have sworn I took his note with me. I must have left it at the library.

"He asked to meet you this late?" Mrs. Wallingford cocked an eyebrow. "Candace has been around, but you, too?"

"It's about Ian Penclosa," I said quickly.

Mrs. Wallingford nodded, but I couldn't miss the raised eyebrow. "Sure." She glanced up the stairs, then back at me. "I'll see if he's still awake. Unless you want to go up without me?"

"Oh, no," I said. "Definitely not. Don't bother him if he's in bed. It's important, or I never would have dropped by like this. Really."

"Wait here a moment."

I understood Mrs. Wallingford's skepticism. It did look peculiar that I'd be coming around to see a Don Juan like Tyrone so late at night. I was certainly testing the cliché about the prim librarian.

Mrs. Wallingford returned down the stairs. "He's not there."

"Asleep, then," I said.

"No. Not there at all. I knocked, and his door opened. He's out. Plus, his key is gone." She pointed at the keys hanging on hooks near the stairs, each with a brass tag dangling from it. The key for room three was missing.

"Thank you." I made my way back to the street.

Tyrone wouldn't have left a note unless it was important. A glance showed his Expedition still in the guest house's driveway. Perhaps he'd walked to the tavern.

A few minutes later, I pushed open the tavern's red vinyl-padded door to a waft of warm beer and onion rings. Marty Robbins played on the sound system. Marty Robbins was a favorite of Orson's, and tavern patrons had long since learned the lyrics to "El Paso" and the fate of its gunslinger and Mexican maiden.

On the way to the bar at the tavern's rear, I passed two booths with patrons. One held Oona, who regularly advertised her insomnia around town by plucking her sweater from her chest and saying things like, "This cardigan? I made it last February when I couldn't sleep." She sipped what looked like a soda and lime, and she wound a skein of wool into a ball. She nodded as I passed. Another booth held a few of the Tohler offspring, digging into chili dogs layered with shreds of cheddar. Betty Larsen sat at the bar, nursing a purple cocktail and making eyes at Orson. She'd been making up to him since her husband died a few years ago. So far, Orson had not taken the bait.

"Have you seen Tyrone Beaudrie?" I asked Orson.

"'Cowboy in the Continental Suit,'" Betty said, nodding at the speaker in the corner. "There's no one who can sing a ballad like Marty Robbins."

Nice try, Betty, I thought.

"You, too, huh?" Orson said. "I thought you were stuck on Sam."

I ignored that. "Tyrone wanted to see me. It seemed important. He wasn't at the guest house, but his car is still there. I thought he might have dropped by."

"Why don't you text him?"

"I don't have his number." Orson was sure being difficult tonight.

"Seems if it was so important, he would have left it."

"Orson, has he been in? Yes or no," I said.

"Nope. Haven't seen him tonight."

"Although personally, I prefer 'A White Sport Coat (and a Pink Carnation),'" Betty said. "So romantic."

I waved goodbye and headed home. Perhaps Tyrone was on a walk. Summer nights were wonderful in Western Oregon, and he might have taken a stroll through the meadow to the millpond, although wandering the woods at night was an unusual pastime for a city dweller like him. Plus, if he'd really needed to see me tonight, he might have made himself easier to find.

Why was his note so urgent? Could that be what had drawn him away?

I supposed I'd find out soon enough. For now, I was going home.

* * *

For the second time in a week, noises in the night woke me. I jolted upright in bed, my heart pounding. Images flew through my head of Ian's inert body on the atrium floor.

I pinched my arm. Yes, I was awake. This was not a dream. I wasn't imagining it.

"Josie!" Sam's voice floated up through my open window.

Sam. Had he come for me at last? I hurried to the window, but the bay window below obscured my view. I rubbed the sleep from my eyes, grabbed my robe, and made for the door. In seconds I was in the library's kitchen.

Sam stood outside the kitchen door's window. "Josie, I need to talk to you."

His tone of voice stopped me halfway across the room. This was no lover's rendezvous. Something serious was up.

I unlocked the door. "Please, come in." It felt strange to be so formal.

He stood, stone-faced, with the mere trace of a smile—a sure sign he was unhappy. "Where were you tonight?" he asked.

"What?"

"Tonight. Where have you been?"

I stepped back and pulled my robe closer. "Sleeping. You woke me up."

"Earlier. Where were you earlier tonight?"

"I visited Lalena," I said. Sam nodded. "Then I went to the meeting at the retreat center." I glanced up to see if he knew about it. He nodded again. "Lots of people saw me there."

"Then what?"

"Come in, if you'd like." I stepped aside to let him enter the kitchen. It gave me a moment to collect myself before relaying the rest of my evening. I didn't want Sam to misunderstand. "I went to look for Tyrone Beaudrie." Sam opened his mouth to reply, but I forged ahead. "Ian Penclosa is missing. Tyrone left me a note saying he had information about him."

"Tyrone Beaudrie? Why would he know anything about Ian?"

"They're both from Baltimore," I said.

"Baltimore."

I nodded.

"Do you have this note?"

Sam was asking me for proof? "You don't believe me," I said. "You think I'm lying."

"I'd like to see the note, please."

"Wait here."

My face stung as I took the service staircase to my apartment. Sam's stony expression hurt more than his flat-out ignoring of me. I checked my pants pockets, but Tyrone's note wasn't there. It wasn't in my purse, either. It was as if it hadn't existed. Slowly, I returned downstairs.

"I can't find the note, but it was there. He stuck it in the door jamb. Ask him, if you don't believe me."

Sam examined my face under the kitchen's bright lights. A stranger would have seen only its impenetrable façade, but I knew a thousand thoughts rushed through his head. He wanted to say something hard, and he didn't know how.

"What is it, Sam?"

"You were seen a few nights ago going into the woods."

The witch's circle. Someone must have spotted me taking Babe Hamilton's linens to be burned. I nodded, and my blood chilled. Something had happened. Something bad.

"You made a fire."

"Yes, I did." What did he want? Sam knew I was a witch. I'd shown him in terms he couldn't deny and apparently couldn't accept, either. Explaining about Babe and Aunt Beata wouldn't help me. Not to mention the fact that Babe had fled town.

"You don't deny it?" Sam asked.

"No." Sam couldn't accept who I was. It hurt, but I couldn't change for him. "No, I don't deny it. Why should I? Yes, I made a fire in the woods. Is that all?"

"We found the remains of a body in the fire pit."

My arms fell to my side. "You found *what*?"

"Josie Way, you're under arrest for the murder of Ian Penclosa."

Chapter Twenty

I wanted to speak, but couldn't. Words frenzied in my head like a cyclone of hornets, but none would come to my throat.

Sam made no move to handcuff me, and he didn't have backup. This was a courtesy to me, I knew. Somehow it only lasered more attention on the incredulous predicament in which I found myself: I had been arrested for murder.

At last, a few words came. "You found Ian Penclosa's body?"

"The medical examiner will confirm it." Sam's gaze was impossible to read. He might have been a statue for all the emotion he showed.

"You don't know, then."

"Lalena tells me Ian is missing. His car is in the driveway, but he hasn't shown up at the This-N-That, and he doesn't answer his phone. You know this."

"Yes."

"You claimed to have seen his body. Inside." Sam

nodded toward the atrium. "Then you put on a charade, asking about him around town."

"It wasn't a charade." When he didn't reply, I added, "You think I set this up. You think I was covering up a murder?" The words might have been stuck in my throat a moment ago, but now they couldn't escape quickly enough. "Why? Why would I do it?"

"It doesn't matter. You were seen going to the woods, and you were out the night he disappeared, the night you said you found him in the atrium."

"No," I said quickly. "No, I wasn't out that night. I was home."

"Josie, people saw you. I have their statements. Besides, you just admitted going to the woods."

"I mean, other than the woods."

Behind Sam, a sheriff's SUV rolled into the driveway, its lights flashing, but no siren. It was really happening. I was really under arrest.

"I'm sorry," Sam whispered, his only display of emotion. "Go upstairs and get dressed."

Then they took me away.

I sat on a hard plastic chair in an interview room in the detention center and waited. I didn't know what I'd expected of jail—iron bars and drunks sleeping off benders?—but this was more like waiting for a meeting in a dingy county building than finding myself in the tank in a film noir. A window with a mirrorlike surface covered one wall. Whether or not an officer watched from the other side was anyone's guess.

As in the movies, however, I did have the chance to

call an attorney. It was the middle of the night. I wouldn't be able to reach anyone until morning. Even then, I didn't know who to call. Lalena, my best friend in Wilfred, might suspect I'd killed her boyfriend. I doubted she'd be eager to set me up with a criminal defense attorney. My family was all the way across the country. I hoped the county's public defender was good.

"Josephine Way?"

A uniformed officer stood in the doorway. She handed me a paper cup of weak coffee. "That's me," I said.

"I'll take you to a cell. You'll be questioned in the morning."

She led me to a stuffy windowless room with a toilet bolted to the wall, and she locked me in with a clank of a thrown bolt.

I would have a lot of time to think that night, because I certainly wouldn't be sleeping. The hum of the jail's ventilation system and the faraway moans of some other poor arrestee didn't help.

Yes, I had been at the witch's circle in the woods, and it was true I'd built a fire. However, I'd burned linens, not a body. I wasn't sure how I was going to explain that I was destroying a spell set by another witch, but I'd have to think of some excuse.

I shifted on the hard mattress.

Even if I'd wanted to burn a body, how could I have hauled a man's corpse through the woods? Unless they thought I'd somehow brought him there alive, then killed him.

And what about seeing Ian in the library's atrium? Was that dream-addled sleep or something more real? Like magic? More specifically, Beata?

No matter what angle I took in thinking over the situation, I arrived at the same conclusion: it was impossible. It was impossible that I was out the night I'd found Ian's body. In fact, finding Ian's body in the atrium—then having it vanish—was also impossible. It was certainly impossible that I'd killed him, then attempted to burn his body.

I'd been a fool to underestimate Beata. In whatever form she took—Babe Hamilton or Lise Bloom or whomever—she wasn't finished with me. Lise had known about the witch's circle. She'd pointed it out when I'd met her on the trail. With Beata's glamour, even in its current weaker form, she might have been able to make me see what she wanted me to see, including an innocent woman with whom I felt an unusual kinship.

I was being set up, and there was only one person who could have done it. A witch. And that witch had to be Aunt Beata.

Chapter Twenty-one

"**Y**ou can be honest with me," the man from the public defender's office told me. "Attorney-client privilege."

I'd been woken that morning by a knock on my cell door just after I'd finally been able to fall asleep. The jail attendant had let in a tall, elderly man in a shiny double-breasted suit he must have bought in the 1980s. He'd paired it with black sneakers and white socks. Whatever his sartorial choices, I eagerly took the latte he handed me.

"George Norton, from the public defender's office." He followed up the coffee cup with a business card.

My experience in jail continued to challenge my expectations. I'd assumed a public defender would be young and inexperienced. I eyed my attorney. Maybe he hadn't been able to get promoted.

Now, our coffee cups drained and my story told, he shook his head. "Why would you be burning a bunch of sheets? And why in the middle of the night? Doesn't make sense. Why not just give them away if they bothered you so much?"

"I had reasons," I said. How to be honest but not stray into magic? If I told him I was a witch, he'd refer me to the state mental hospital. "They came from someone I didn't like."

"So you took them to the woods. In the middle of the night." He let out his breath in a half sigh, half snort. "No, that won't fly. I can't help you if you won't tell me the truth."

"That is the truth. I could make up some kind of story, but it would be just that—a story."

"How about the murder weapon, then? Where's that?"

Was this a trap? "I don't know how he was killed. I'm just as puzzled as you."

"If they find the murder weapon in your apartment, you're in trouble."

I was already in trouble. The case against me was nearly impenetrable. "What about Ian's wheelchair?" I asked.

"Say what?"

"Ian Penclosa was paraplegic. He couldn't get around without a wheelchair. Finding it might lead to . . . new evidence."

As soon as the words left my mouth, I feared any new evidence would only serve as another brick in the fortress-like case against me. A witch powerful enough to materialize this kind of case could manage a few fingerprints on a wheelchair.

The attorney swatted dismissively. "Could be at the bottom of the river by now. It hardly matters, given what they already have against you."

I'd been an idiot to forget Babe Hamilton so easily, to think I'd driven her away simply by breaking her spell on the linens. She'd taken it as an opportunity to silence me for good.

The attorney leaned back. "We can't say the death was an accident. Not with the fire, etcetera. Can we make a case for self-defense?"

"I didn't kill him," I said. "You have to believe me. I know it looks like I did, but, I tell you, I've only been trying to find him."

"And why is that?"

"Because he's my good friend's boyfriend, and she was worried. She couldn't get in touch with him. She wanted me to locate him and find out what was wrong."

The attorney jabbed the air with a forefinger. "Motive. Right there. You killed him for the sisterhood."

"No!" I groaned with frustration. "I'm innocent. I told you."

He leaned toward me. "Let me make this very clear. You have been documented trying to locate Ian Penclosa. You reported finding him dead, but no body was recovered. You were seen late at night going into the woods where Mr. Penclosa's body was found. Then you made a show of continuing to look for him. And your only excuse is that you were looking out for a friend and that you didn't like some sheets, so you burned them, exactly where Penclosa's body was found."

"I'm innocent," I said, my voice faltering.

"Like I haven't heard those words before." When I

didn't reply—what could I say, after all?—he continued. "Tell me everything. The truth. I can't help you unless I know exactly what happened."

At least there were books in prison. Maybe they'd let me volunteer as the librarian. I thought about Rodney. He was a resourceful cat and would find a new home. However, my family would be crushed. How many years would I be sentenced for?

The door to the interview room opened, and a sheriff's deputy—not Sam; I hadn't seen him since he'd handed me off at the library—stood, the door behind him ajar.

"You're free to go," the deputy said.

"What?" the attorney and I said at the same time.

"You'll need to stay in touch. You're still under suspicion."

"Why, may I ask, is my client to be released?" the attorney said. He'd sat straighter and almost appeared court-worthy.

I shot him a dirty look. Shouldn't he be happy for me?

"Evidence that pertained to her arrest was disproven," the deputy said.

"What would this evidence be?" the attorney said.

"I repeat, Ms. Way is still a suspect and may be detained again."

"You didn't answer my question," the attorney said.

Speechless, I watched the two men talk. What was going on?

"Ian Penclosa," the deputy said. "He's been found. Alive."

Chapter Twenty-two

Roz greeted me at the library's service entrance, where I'd been hoping to sneak in. She must have been lying in wait. "Are you all right?" she asked, genuine concern in her voice.

Word about my situation had already got around. Someone might have seen the sheriff's SUV last night with its lights flashing and even spotted my form in the its back seat. From there, it would have taken a quick call to Roz in the morning to double-check that I wasn't at the library, then a tap into Wilfred's vast intelligence network, which included operatives throughout the county. I wouldn't be surprised if someone's uncle's neighbor was a janitor at the detention center.

Behind Roz, the books murmured a soothing welcome, as calming as bath water.

"Give me half an hour for a shower and a change of clothing, and I'll be down," I said. I wouldn't mind grabbing a sandwich, either. Even if the jail's powdered scrambled eggs and cold toast had tempted me, I couldn't eat my breakfast.

When I reemerged into the library, clean but bleary-eyed, a welcoming committee of library regulars greeted me.

"Hello, jailbird," Duke said. He'd clearly left in the middle of a job—something greasy, too, although his hair still wore its crisp Brylcreemed wave.

"You'll find prison more comfortable than jail," Desmond said. Rumor had it he had personal experience with the justice system, but until now had never acknowledged it publicly. "But don't mess with the tattoos. Had a buddy who got a terrible infection."

"Who's to say I'm going to prison?" I said. "I haven't done anything wrong."

Mrs. Garlington stepped forward, a sheaf of sheet music under one arm. "Honey, you look terrible. I'll have Darla send up something from the café."

Roz's earlier concern vanished, and she regarded me with narrowed eyes. "You could have let me know you wouldn't be here. I had to open up the library myself when I heard patrons pounding on the kitchen door. I made coffee, cleared out the book return, unlocked the—"

"Stop!" I said. "Just let me through to Circulation, please."

"Unacceptable," came a voice from the rear. Wanda.

I screwed my eyes shut and opened them again. She was still there. I was not up for this.

"Clearly and completely." The gathering parted to make way for her. "Wilfred does not need a suspected killer running its library. The materials in the children's room are bad enough, but we will not have our residents exposed to a murderous witch with—"

"A what?" I said.

"Just because someone's been called in once or twice doesn't mean—" Desmond started.

Once or twice? "It was a mistake," I said. "They know it. They released me, see?"

Wanda folded her arms over her chest. "Police don't arrest people for nothing. You could be back in lock-up by dinner."

Roz cleared the way to my side. "Everyone, go back to whatever you were doing. Josie needs to get to work."

"I'll see you at the trustees' meeting tonight," Wanda said. "We'll put this to rest once and for all."

My head hurt. I hadn't prepared a thing for the trustees' meeting. I'd have to rely on the trustees' common sense to deal with Wanda. I let Roz lead me to the circulation desk, where I fell into my chair. My instinct was to hide upstairs, but I wouldn't let this situation get me down—or at least, I wouldn't show it.

"Sam arrested you, did he?" Roz's voice was concerned and soft. Also borderline nosy. "That couldn't have been easy."

I raised my eyes to hers. "None of it was easy, and the sooner it's cleared up, the better."

She read my tone and retreated to the conservatory to work on her manuscript.

My next move was clear. I didn't even hesitate. I had a hunch I knew who the body in the burn circle was. Once I confirmed it, I'd simply need to find out who killed him, and why. All with a rival witch breathing down my back.

I'd hoped to have a moment alone at the circulation desk, but it wasn't to be—at least, not until Roz took over at noon. Instead, Circulation was crowded with patrons, many of them brand new to the library and clutching random books they'd grabbed from the shelves simply to have the opportunity for face time with someone recently arrested for murder. *Me.*

A book on budgie raising twittered under the arm of a pimple-faced boy who stared baldly at me. *Building and Detailing Model Aircraft* whispered "choose me" in my ear.

"Raising budgies, are you?" I asked.

"Uh-huh," the boy replied, unable to tear his gaze from my face. What did he think he'd see? Hatchet scars?

"The library has a great collection of books on other hobbies, too, like"—I raised my eyes, as if searching my brain—"building model airplanes."

The boy's attention snapped from pondering murder to what I'd just said. "No kidding?"

"Upstairs, at the end of the hall on your right." I pointed to the book under his arm. "You can leave that here."

He dropped the book on my desk—it landed with happy chirping—and scampered out. One down, and, judging from the line that had formed, several dozen to go. I groaned silently.

"Stay to the right, please," I said. "Let people come in if they want to browse New Releases."

Half the crowd moved to the right to get a private audience with me, however brief, and half dispersed to pretend to scan new releases.

After an hour of fielding questions about books patrons didn't actually want to read, questions they'd made up simply to look me over, I'd had enough. I stood. "Thank you, everyone, for coming in today. My guess is some of you might not be here to use the library, but instead want to see me. You heard I was arrested last night."

Silence greeted me, but I'd definitely captured their attention.

"Let me give you the story firsthand. After that, I have work to do, and I'd like people who are simply curious to go home. Do we have an agreement?"

Slowly, heads nodded through the crowd. A few people dropped their randomly fetched books on nearby shelves.

"Last night, late, Sam Wilfred arrested me for the murder of Ian Penclosa. He said someone had seen me going into the woods, and later an anonymous caller reported a burnt body near where I was spotted."

Oohs and *aahs* spread through Circulation and into the atrium. A few people nudged ahead for a better position.

"It's no secret that I've been looking for Ian, but it wasn't to kill him." To my horror, I was getting choked up. I paused to calm my breathing. "And, thankfully, Ian is still alive. So I was released." I let out a long breath.

The crowd froze for a moment, taking this all in. Then, someone spoke. "That doesn't leave you off the hook. By your own admission, you were hanging out in the woods."

"Plus," an older man said, "there's still a body."

"I'm not certain who was found in the woods or how and why he died. I had nothing to do with it," I said. "I want to know as much you do—more, really."

A mother took a long look at me, then pulled in her school-aged daughter close. "Come on, honey. We're going home." She shot me an accusatory glance and left.

"What if the dead guy is someone you've been seen with?" a man asked. He leaned against a shelf, arms folded. I remembered him checking out a series of automotive repair manuals last spring.

"You mean, what if it's Tyrone Beaudrie?" I asked. I, too, had the same suspicion. "Has anyone seen him lately?"

"You were looking for him," Ruth Littlewood said. I hadn't noticed her come in.

"I was. Yes. And I didn't find him."

"He wasn't at the café this morning," someone said.

"Or at the Empress," someone else added. "I heard some of his crew complaining about needing him. He was a no-show."

I pondered this only a split second before I asked, "Ian. Where is he?"

Chapter Twenty-three

As was true at the library, at the café I was the center of attention. The moment I entered, forks were dropped and voices stilled. Chairs scraped the linoleum as diners turned to look at me. From behind the cash register, Darla mouthed, "Tuna melt?" and I nodded.

"Has anyone seen Ian?" I asked. "I know he's around."

"He hasn't been here," a Tohler volunteered.

"Or at the This-N-That," Patty said.

"He might be home." That comment came from a girl's voice. Buffy stepped forward. "Me and Thor could find him."

"For a fee," several people said.

I opened my purse and fished out a twenty-dollar bill. "Here you go. I need results before"—I glanced at the cat clock on the wall, the clock with the tail as a pendulum. Strange that Wanda hadn't insisted yet on its removal—"before two o'clock. Think you can do that?"

A cape and a blur of pink glitter made for the door. Buffy and Thor were on the job.

Buffy and Thor found me at the library not long after lunch, Thor twirling his cape in one hand. I was in my office, finishing my tuna melt and ruminating on the disaster in which I now found myself. The puzzle was coming together, and I didn't like where the pieces lay.

An unidentified dead man had been found in the witch's circle. Tyrone Beaudrie was missing. Ian Penclosa had vanished and reappeared. Tyrone and Ian were from the same hometown. Could Ian have killed him?

"We got results," Buffy said.

"An hour early," Thor added. "How about a bonus?"

I set my bread crust on my plate, and Rodney roused himself from his nap on the windowsill long enough to sniff at the remains.

"I paid more than twice your usual rates," I said.

"This was a rush job," Buffy pointed out. "It deserved a premium."

"No messing around. Where's Ian?" I said. "It's a matter of life and death." *Possibly Tyrone's*, I thought, *but the kids didn't have to know that.* "Like in the Camelot classic comic books you've been reading, Thor." The library had a full collection. They'd been Sam's when he was a boy. "Sir Lancelot didn't monkey around on his horse asking for money. He got things done."

Thor let his cape drop from his hands. "All right."

"All right, what? Where is he?"

Buffy and Thor looked at each other. Finally, Buffy spoke. "He's at home."

That was it? Ian was home? "Alone?"

"You mean, was he, like, all lovey-dovey with Lalena?" Buffy asked.

"Was he by himself?" I repeated. I corrected my tone of voice to be less short. It wasn't Buffy and Thor's fault I was suspected of homicide, and, on top of that, had had very little sleep.

"Yes," Thor said. "We knocked on his door and asked if he wanted a car wash, and we didn't see anyone else."

"He said his car was fine," Buffy added. "But he kept looking around, like he thought someone was going to get him."

Someone like the sheriff, maybe, I wondered. "Thanks, you two."

After they ran off, I went to find Roz at Circulation. She was perusing a home-decorating magazine.

"What do you think of these curtains? Too busy?" She pointed at a photo of floor-to-ceiling pink chintz drapes. "Lyndon would appreciate the botanical theme."

"Perfect for a romance author," I said. I took a fortifying breath. "I need to take the afternoon off." I braced myself for Roz's disapproving glare.

"Okay," she said absently.

My jaw gaped. "You're fine with it?" Although I was Roz's boss on paper, she somehow usually ended up gaining the upper hand.

"Sure." She absently flipped the page. "You won't have much personal time in the pen. Might as well enjoy freedom while you've got it."

I resisted the urge to swipe her hand fan and tap her on the skull, and I made my way over the river and down the hill to the Magnolia Rolling Estates.

Fingers crossed it was not to visit a murderer.

Ian's van was still parked in its same spot in the driveway. Neither light nor movement showed in his trailer's windows. Yet Buffy and Thor had said he was home.

I hesitated before coming closer. If my guess was right that Tyrone's was the body found in the woods, Ian was the logical killer. However, I couldn't imagine him wheeling his chair through the fern-choked trail with a body over his shoulder. He might have lured Tyrone to the woods and killed him there, but even that was a stretch. If there was any bad blood between the men, there's little chance Tyrone would have taken Ian's bait.

Then there was the fact that Ian had presented himself at the sheriff's office to prove he was alive. If he had killed Tyrone, why would he come out of hiding to get me off the hook?

My Aunt Beata was behind this. I was sure of it. However, my guess was that her style was more to drive people to their deaths, not to murder them outright. She may have latched onto another man's crime to have me put away. If so, it was possible that man was Ian.

I gingerly walked up the ramp to the front door and raised my fist to knock. Before my hand made contact, the door opened. I faced Ian through the screen.

"Josie! I'm so glad you're all right," Ian said.

"You are?"

"Come in." He rolled his chair back and motioned for me to enter. He certainly wasn't acting like a murderer. "Sit down."

I pushed open the screen door and took a seat on the couch. "Where have you been?"

"I had to let them know I was alive," Ian said, his words coming in a rush. "When I found out you were arrested, that is." He rolled back an inch. "For my murder."

"How did you know? You still haven't said where you were."

"I was hiding."

I waited for more. The detective novels I loved so much recommended silence as a way to elicit further response, but it didn't seem to be working right now. "Where? Lalena looked everywhere for you."

The mention of Lalena's name worked. "I felt so bad disappearing like that. It was for her own good. If she'd known. . . ."

Again, giving him space to fill the void was a fail. "If she'd known what? Ian, stop horsing around. Where have you been, and why?" I leaned forward and lobbed my biggest bomb. "Did you kill Tyrone Beaudrie?"

The shock on Ian's face was real. He had no idea Tyrone was dead. Of course, I wasn't completely sure, either.

"Who's Tyrone Beaudrie?" he said.

Now I was the flummoxed one. In the distance, a lawn mower started up. Outside, the world rolled on with its routines of grass cutting, dinner prep, and children playing. Inside, tangled threads of fear and murder waited to be put straight. Ian's scar whitened in the light, then faded back to pale pink as he turned his head.

"Let's start at the beginning," I said. "A week and a half ago, you dropped out of sight. When construction started at the Empress." Or was that a coincidence?

His nod confirmed that I was on target so far. To me, Ian had always appeared reserved, although I caught hints of a boyish vulnerability. Clearly, Lalena did, too, or she wouldn't be so smitten with him. He opened up now. Whether it was design or simply exhaustion, I didn't know.

"You want the beginning? Here's the beginning." He examined the hand resting on the wheel of his chair, then raised his eyes to mine. "I grew up in a rough neighborhood in Baltimore, and I fell in with the wrong crowd."

"As happens," I said, hoping this would encourage him further.

"My home life was rough. My mother was gone, and Dad wasn't around much, either. I guess I was looking for family."

Despite myself, my heart softened. "I see."

He looked away. "Me and a few other kids worked for a gang who ran a protection racket."

"A protection racket?"

"Some older men had set it up. They told businesses in the neighborhood they had to pay a monthly fee, or they'd find their stores vandalized. You know, windows broken, goods stolen—things like that. My role was to collect payments and, when needed, break a few windows." He drummed his fingers on the arm of his wheelchair. "I'm not proud of it. This was before my injury, of course."

I didn't want to interrupt his narrative, so I simply nodded.

"One of the shop owners had a used bookstore. He was different from the rest. Other business owners either paid us quickly without making eye contact, or they were openly hostile." Ian snorted. "Not that I blamed them. But Mr. Ehrenberg was different. When he saw me looking at a stack of books on his counter, he showed one to me. It had engravings of old ships." Ian's voice sounded faraway now, lost in a long-ago memory.

I understood that love of books. I knew the wonder of discovering that a flat bundle of bound paper could reveal whole worlds teeming with sights, sounds, and emotion. It still thrilled me.

"Mr. Ehrenberg turned my life around. He made me see that so much more was possible than a life of being a stoolie in someone's protection racket. I couldn't thank him enough. I. . . ."

Again, the fading out. Then I understood. "He's not . . . he's passed, hasn't he?"

"Yes. He died." Ian's voice raised in pitch. "Apparently my bosses thought he should pay a bit more, and when he demurred, they trashed his shop. He had a heart attack. Died."

"They killed him." It was a statement, not a question.

"Indirectly," Ian said. "His heart couldn't stand the strain."

There was more to this story. This time, my patience paid off.

"I couldn't stick around," Ian said. "I had to get out of there."

"You couldn't just quit?" I asked.

He shook his head. "I might have been able to quit, maybe, but Mr. Ehrenberg's money had disappeared. I suspect my boss stole it. To hide it from the others, he accused me."

"You didn't take it," I said with certainty.

"Steal from Mr. Ehrenberg? I couldn't." Ian's voice was incredulous. He held up a hand before I could protest that this was, in fact, what he'd been doing all along, although in someone else's name. "I know what you're going to say. After I left, I sent money to his widow whenever I could. Now she's gone, too."

"You had to leave town."

"Yes. I changed my name and moved across the country. This was years ago. The love of books Mr. Ehrenberg had instilled in me grew, and I ended up buying and selling them, just as he did, but without a storefront. Until I found the This-N-That."

It started to come together now. "When the construction crew came to town, you saw one of your old gang." Wilfred must be everyone's bolt-hole, including Tyrone Beaudrie's, an alias, not the name under which Ian had known him. I remembered his talk of a new life.

"I did. A huge shock. I didn't expect to see him in construction, but it's Byron, all right. I'd been safe for so many years. I never expected to see him again."

"Where did you go?" Wilfred was tiny. If he'd have stayed here, Tyrone-slash-Byron would have seen him.

"Forest Grove. One of the professors at the university had died and left a huge book collection, and I'd agreed to help catalog it, get it ready to sell. When I saw Byron, I told them I'd start right away. I left a quick voicemail for Lalena and took a taxi within the hour."

I looked around. Ian's home was tranquil and pleasantly cluttered, as I imagined a rare books vendor's home would be. He had a strong arms and torso—he needed them to propel himself in his chair all day—but I didn't sense violence. He'd fled Baltimore instead of fighting his boss. He wasn't a killer.

As I prepared my next words, I prayed I was right. "You didn't murder him?"

Ian started. "Absolutely not. I don't want him to know I still exist, let alone confront him. No way." He squinted. "You say he's dead? Are you sure?"

"I think so. A man's body was found in the woods. There's a strong chance it's him, and, if you're right, he was here under a pseudonym. Tyrone Beaudrie. He wasn't at the guest house last night, and he hasn't shown up for work."

"The guest house, huh?" Ian shook his head in disbelief. "He's dead?" His puzzlement morphed into a wide smile, then dimmed. "Someone killed him."

"From what you say, I imagine he has his enemies." I remembered Tyrone's seductive grace, his sly double-talk. If not a gang boss, his murderer might well have been a jealous ex-girlfriend.

"You were arrested for murder. *His* murder, not mine," Ian said.

"And you heard about it somehow."

He shrugged. "The windows were open. Someone outside was talking about how I was dead, and you'd been arrested for killing me. I knew I'd better make it known I was alive—at least to the sheriff's office. I didn't understand at the time, but now it's starting to come together." He shook his head. "Wow." Then, "I need to see Lalena. It's safe now that Byron is dead."

Indeed, a sense of calm seemed to have settled over Ian. I rose.

"I hope she'll understand why I had to vanish like that." He looked at me with a question in his gaze.

"If you're as honest with her as you've been with me, I predict she'll forgive all."

My words were upbeat, but my mood was not. I had a lot to figure out, and it was becoming increasingly clear that my life depended on it.

Chapter Twenty-four

That night the library was noisy with Wilfredians gathered for the trustees' meeting. The atrium looked as it always had: the Eastlake table with its vase of dahlias lovingly arranged by Lyndon adorned the center; the cupola's stained glass sparkled like jewels under the moonlight; bookshelves full of happy books lined the former mansion's rooms.

The big difference was that trustees' meetings didn't usually even draw the full complement of trustees, let alone most of Wilfred. Tonight's was not one of those meetings.

Ruth Littlewood banged her gavel on the lectern. "May I have your attention, please? Quiet, everyone."

As Wilfredians usually did when Ruth spoke, they obeyed.

"We're going to bypass our usual agenda of budgetary review, etcetera, and go straight to a subject vital to the health of our community: cats."

The crowd grumbled, but I did hear a few *huzzah*s.

"Cats are a menace to society." Ruth cleared her voice, and her words picked up power. "They are an enemy to birds, and many people are allergic to them. They appear cuddly, but in fact have deadly sharp claws. In short, the house cat is a greatly underestimated threat."

I raised my hand, and Ruth nodded. I wasn't sure if we were following Robert's Rules of Order, but I intended to take part in this discussion. "Perhaps you'd like to be more specific. This meeting isn't about cats, but about the suitability of having books featuring cats in the library's children's section."

"Corrected," Ruth said.

Wanda harrumphed from her front-row seat. She clutched a sheaf of papers, and an overhead projector sat on the front table. This could be a long night.

Mona tapped my shoulder. "May I sit behind you?" She held a small bottle and a bundle wrapped in a towel, most likely her latest foster charge.

"Sure," I said. "We're just getting started."

Mona unwrapped the bundle to reveal a tabby kitten. Not helpful. I turned again to the front of the room and tried to make my back as wide as possible to hide the kitten.

"Sorry," she whispered, "but I couldn't leave her home."

Ruth waved a hand toward Wanda. "I'd like to introduce a member of the community to explain these views further. I believe everyone knows Wanda, the new caretaker at the retreat center."

Wanda set her bundle of papers on the lectern, then plugged the projector into an extension cord leading into the kitchen. She wore a crisply pressed but decades-old blue suit and had even applied a smudge of red lipstick. She was all business. She slipped on a pair of reading glasses.

"Thank you, fellow Wilfredians, for your attention to this very important issue. Currently, the library has a plethora of books in the children's section featuring cats, often in primary roles. These books portray cats as sympathetic, cuddly, and occasionally even wise beings. In fact, they are dangerous creatures that should have never been domesticated."

She placed a slide on the projector, and the cartoon image of a hissing cat in a baby's cradle appeared on the portable screen. Next to the cradle were several bottles ostentatiously labeled *allergy medicine*. An arrow pointed out the window with the words *dead birds* printed next to it.

"Not a bad drawing," Duke said from somewhere behind me.

"I propose we remove these dangerous books from our publicly funded space, lest children get the wrong idea."

Before Wanda could finish her sentence, the projector went dead. I caught a flash of black fur darting through the kitchen doorway. *Rodney*. I closed my eyes and groaned.

"That cat did it, didn't he?" Wanda said. "I made my point."

"Removing books is no way to deal with this," Patty said. Bless her. "I have grandkids, and I want them to learn about all sorts of things."

"I'm not saying books with cats should be eliminated," Wanda said. "You can read these books to your grandchildren if you want to. That way, you'll be able to expose them to the reality of cats in a responsible fashion."

My blood pressure was rising to rival a steam engine, but I felt more incredulous than angry. Before I could reply, Duke jumped in. "Great idea," he said. "I'd like to see books about birds taken out of the library, too. All of them, not just the books for kids."

Ruth Littlewood shot to her feet, her birdwatching binoculars swaying on her chest. "What?"

"You think cats are a menace?" Duke said. "Look at birds. They wake you up in the morning with their racket, they nest in buildings, and they crap on cars. Birds should be eliminated. Ever wonder why I eat so much chicken? To cut down their numbers."

Lyndon rose. This was surprising. "Birds also steal fruit in the garden. I have to put nets on the blueberries."

"I never," Ruth said. "This is censorship, plain and simple."

Mrs. Tohler rose. "While we're at it, I have a problem with leaf blowers. People are too lazy to pick up a rake so they fire up noisy, gas-guzzling contraptions, instead? How is that good for society?"

I doubted we had children's books that featured motorized lawn care equipment, but before I could say anything, an older woman grasped her cane and stood. "I'm offended by depictions of the elderly in books. Sure, my hair is white and I use a cane, but that doesn't mean I'm helpless. If you ask me, every book containing the word *doddering* should be removed."

It was time to step in. I stood. "As Wilfred's librarian, I'd like to—"

Wanda pounded a fist on the lectern and pointed at me. "You're going to take the word of a woman accused of murder?"

Wow. That was a low blow. I drew a deep breath. "As I said, as Wilfred's librarian, I believe we can find compromise. We all have opinions about what's right and wrong. A library isn't a boxing ring where one view wins over another. A library is about sharing different perspectives and learning about them."

I looked up to measure Wanda's reaction to, what seemed to me, a logical argument, and found her staring straight at Mona. *Uh-oh*.

"What is that?" she said, her voice menacing.

Mona's jaw tensed. "Don't threaten me."

"I asked you what you have in your lap." Wanda's voice came low and sinister.

Mona defiantly flipped the towel to hide the kitten she was bottle nursing. "I don't know what you're talking about."

Wanda removed her reading glasses and crept, eyes narrowed, toward Mona. This was the kind of walk Rodney affected when he stalked prey, like the ponytail elastic he regularly chased through my apartment.

"It's a cat. I saw it." Wanda practically growled.

Mona lifted her chin. "And what if it is? Cats hurt no one, and that goes double for a children's book about a cat."

Now Wanda faced Mona head-on, and the look in her eyes could have frozen rain into icicles. "You have no idea. Even if children don't read these books, the covers alone influence them. Merely by looking at them they get the idea that cats are harmless. Cute, even."

"Parents keep an eye on what their children read. If there's anything to explain, like that cats don't actually wear striped hats and speak in rhyme, they can," Mona said. "What's the big deal?"

"Imagine this," Wanda said. "A parent determines that reading fiction about cats isn't what's best for their child. Then the kid sees another kid carrying around something like"—from her sheaf of papers, she extracted the photocopy of a book cover featuring a cat drinking tea—"like this, and the first kid gets the mistaken idea that cats are perfectly innocent. If one child can check them out, it hurts every child."

Defiant, Mona slowly unveiled the kitten. The tabby's eyes were closed, and her tiny paws, with their little pink toe beans, made biscuits as she suckled the bottle. "Cats spread love," Mona said. "And comfort. They're beautiful. There's nothing more soothing than reading with a purring cat on your lap. For some people, they're the only friends they have. Just because you don't approve of cats doesn't mean you have the right to foist your beliefs on everyone else."

Wanda turned away. She lived alone at the retreat center. Other than Ruth, she hadn't seemed to make many friends. Perhaps Mona had hit a nerve.

When Wanda turned back, I saw I'd been mistaken. She wasn't sad; she was enraged. Her eyes bulged, and her face was as red as Lyndon's prize-winning beet from the county fair. She gulped air as if to speak, but no words came out.

Ruth quickly grasped the situation. "This meeting

will be postponed. Wanda, everyone, thank you for your thoughts. We'll reconvene in a few days."

She left the podium and led Wanda by the shoulders to a chair. People slowly filed out of the atrium, and I retreated to my office to give Ruth and Wanda privacy. When I reemerged, they were gone, and the library was once again empty.

Ruth wouldn't delay rescheduling the trustees' meeting. By then, I'd have to have a plan. That was, if I wasn't in jail.

Chapter Twenty-five

The next day at the library, I hid in my office, half-heartedly doing admin work and pondering last night's trustees' meeting.

I couldn't think about a strategy for the trustees' meeting now—not while a potential arrest for murder hung over my head. If it wasn't for Ian's courage in contacting the sheriff's office, I'd still be behind bars.

Once Roz closed the library for the day, I emerged from my office and waved goodbye to her, then circled the library, drawing curtains and snapping off lights. Thankfully, there were no meetings tonight. I'd have time to think. And plan.

First, I needed to get to the bottom of the identity of the body found in the woods. My working theory was that it was Tyrone Beaudrie. Was I right?

I picked up my phone and called the Wallingford Guest House. "Is Tyrone Beaudrie there?" I asked. "It's Josie Way." I winced as I identified myself. After a day of being a spectacle, I was full up.

"Hello, Josie. No, no Tyrone. If you'll excuse me, Sheriff Wilfred is here."

I hung up. Sam was at the guest house, and Tyrone was not. Sam was on the same trail I was. How long would it be before he arrested me for killing Tyrone? I had one more call to make.

"Hello, Patty?" If anyone was tapped into the Wilfred grapevine, it was Patty. "Have you seen Tyrone Beaudrie anywhere?"

"Not since yesterday." Her voice was almost gleeful. "Word is he's missing. Might even be the body they found in the woods. The sheriff just stopped by the guest house to try to track him down. On that note, how's life on the outside? Some trustees' meeting, huh?"

I made an excuse about how I was tired and couldn't talk, and I dropped to the armchair in my apartment. Rodney leapt to my lap and, purring, circled to lie down.

People had seen me wandering town when I'd actually been home. I'd found Ian lying, dead, on the atrium's floor—yet it hadn't been him. Or anyone.

I'd burned Babe Hamilton's charmed linens in the woods, and a body showed up in the same place a few days later. More than mere human interference was going on here. Bad magic was involved—I felt it. Aunt Beata was behind it. I was sure.

But that didn't make sense, either. If she'd wanted me gone, why not simply do away with me? According to my grandmother's letter, Grandma had tied up the bulk of Beata's power and banished her. Beata clearly had enough magic left to block mine—at least temporarily. She may have been feeding off the magic she'd suppressed in me, as well. Given that her gift was glamour, she could use that siphoned magic to make people—including me—see what she wanted us to see. She could appear as anyone.

I remembered Lise Bloom on the forest path, looking at me with eyes that were oddly familiar.

Fatigue weighed on me, but every hour counted. If Aunt Beata was orchestrating my murder rap, as I believed, she would know I'd been freed from police custody, and she would be planning something to put me away again.

My grandmother thought Beata would come to me to break the spell binding her magic. If so, putting me behind bars wasn't a smart move. I couldn't figure it out.

There was only one way to get the answers I needed, and that was to go directly to Beata. I didn't like it, but if I was going to clear my name and put a stop to the campaign to make me out as a murderer, I was going to have to do it.

Besides, I reminded myself, I was the more powerful witch. Less experienced, but with more raw magic—at least, I should be.

Rodney's purring practically vibrated within me. Then it stopped. He gazed up as if trying to read my mind.

"It will be okay," I told him. "I'm not afraid. You'll see."

He continued to stare.

"We have no choice."

Rodney jumped off my lap and leapt to the window sill.

"I have to do it, kitten. It's this or a conviction for murder."

* * *

I slid the trunk of my grandmother's letters from under the bed. Rodney jumped onto the cotton coverlet that had replaced the quilt Beata had charmed, and he tapped a paw near me.

"We're going to do it, baby," I told him.

He backed away and settled down.

I opened the trunk and thrust my hands into the letters. This time, they lay cold, but beneath them, my grandmother's grimoire burned hot. As my fingers reached it, magical energy surged into my hands, causing me to inhale sharply and raising goosebumps up my arms.

For a moment, I let the energy metabolize, and I looked around my bedroom, hoping it wouldn't be for the last time. Here was the tall walnut headboard with its Victorian spindles and carvings. There was my nightstand, bare but for a vase holding one glorious scarlet dahlia. I knelt on a rag rug. Across the room was a window that looked across the garden to Big House, and Sam. My heart ached.

I lifted the grimoire onto the bed, and Rodney padded over to sniff its edges. The scent of fresh rosemary and verbena—impossible so many years later, but present nonetheless—wafted into the room. The smell of my grandmother.

I knew books. I loved books. In my years as a librarian—first at the Library of Congress, then at Wilfred—hundreds of thousands of books had passed through my hands, sharing everything from Victorian household hints and Chinese travelogues to histories of snake charmers and bluegrass song lyrics. But this one, my grandmother's book of spells, was like no other.

Every word, every sprig of dried thyme, every sketch of the moon's phases was redolent of my grandmother and pulsed with magic. I opened the grimoire. Its pages began to tremble on their own and flipped slowly forward, then back, then sighed and lay flat. I lowered my fingers to the opened page and jerked them back at the heat, which rippled orange-yellow over the page's surface. Slowly, I lowered my hand again and let the energy surge into me.

Spell to Summon a Witch, the page was titled. Voices—not just my grandmother's, but several women's voices—recited the spell together. Words—*sing, cast, moon, wind*—swirled around me. Were these the voices of my grandmother's mother, and her mother, and hers? Perhaps my voice would join theirs someday, as well. Not too soon, I hoped.

As the voices read the spell, Rodney's eyes half-closed, and his purr rose. Then he did something I'd never heard him do before: underneath his rolling purr, a growl edged in. I moved my hand away. I was at once exhilarated and terrified.

When the reading was complete, the grimoire closed on its own, green-gold energy flowing into it and vanishing. Now I knew what to do to draw Aunt Beata to me.

I couldn't do it here, at the library. I couldn't risk Beata's magic souring the library—or worse. That said, the library's books fueled my magic. Without them, I was still a witch, but I existed like a car without gas. Even a mighty jet engine is nothing without fuel.

The witch's circle. I could go there. I was sure Beata had something to do with the body Sam had found there, and her energy would linger in the rocks and trees. I'd be far enough from the library that she couldn't infect my world. As far as energy went, I would bring *Grimm's Fairy Tales*, the most powerful book I possessed aside from the grimoire.

I would summon Beata, and she would appear. A foreboding shiver ran through me. I was the stronger witch, I reminded myself. As long as I didn't do anything stupid, she couldn't harm me.

Chapter Twenty-six

The moon drew a pale sliver on the velvet night. I clutched *Grimm's Fairy Tales* for comfort. Was I an idiot for summoning a witch I knew was out to get me? Yet, what other option did I have?

To protect myself, I had to confront Beata. To confront her, I had to call up every whisper of magic I possessed and keep my wits sharp. I yawned, then shook my head and yanked my eyes wide. I still hadn't recovered from my night in jail.

Although I hadn't asked him, Rodney had followed me. He padded silently at my side, and I was grateful for his company.

"Here we are, baby," I told him. "I'm doing the right thing, aren't I?"

Rodney ignored me and settled on a fallen log, curling his tail around him.

"You don't have to be here." I knelt to kiss the top of his head. "It will be dangerous. You'd be safer at home."

He responded by tucking his paws under him in classic cat loaf position. He was staying put.

I filled my lungs with night air and slowly released it. Far off, an owl hooted. Otherwise, it was unnaturally quiet here. No crickets, not the merest crackling in the underbrush. The air was still.

I lit a taper and tipped it to drip wax onto a rock in the middle of the fire pit I'd built when I burned Babe's linens, a mere three nights ago. Its center had been thoroughly raked and swept for evidence, but the police tape, if there had been any, was gone. I steadied the taper in the melted wax, and Rodney leapt from the log to join me. My heart, formerly thumping at a parade-level volume, steadied.

I stood tall, *Grimm's Fairy Tales* at my feet, feeding me energy. I faced east. "Wind, with the force of gales that send ships over oceans, lend me your protection." A breeze rose, ruffling my hair before subsiding.

I turned toward the south. Was that a rustle I heard near the trail? I scanned the dark but saw nothing. "Fire, you foster life with the sun, stirring seeds into fields of grain, rousing an acorn into a mighty oak. Lend me your protection." The candle's flame stretched thin and tall, then shrank.

I turned again, this time toward the west. "Water, you are the great mother, giving birth and holding our emotion. Lend me your protection." Wet drops, impossible but present nonetheless, touched my hands.

One more convocation. I faced north. "Earth. Your body nurtures the roots of mighty trees and grounds us all. Lend me your protection." Below my feet, the ground trembled.

"Elements of the universe, protect me." I dropped my hands.

With that, a dome of opalescent light rose around Rodney and me, infusing shimmer into the air surrounding us. Despite its translucence, I felt the dome's protection as if it were cast of steel. Nothing could hurt me here. No bad magic could enter, of that I was certain.

Now for the spell from my grandmother's grimoire. Closing my eyes, at first I strained to remember the words, and then they flowed without effort. Strangely, the words transmuted from English to another language as they left my lips. Scottish Gaelic? Whatever it was, I intuitively understood it.

I hesitated before the spell's final words, but I had to say them. It was now or never. "Her name is Beata."

I tensed. The forest's silence shattered as crows, cawing and flapping their wings, alit in the trees around me. Their cries were loud enough that I flattened my palms to my ears. Rodney growled and crouched low. Seconds stretched to minutes, and the minutes weighed heavily.

I was safe beneath the dome of protection. I knew that. But it took everything I had to stay calm.

Then the cawing stopped. The crows seemed to melt away. Just outside the dome, barely six feet from me, a woman appeared. It was not Babe Hamilton—or Lise Bloom. I'd never seen her before. Her long golden-red hair moved around her face as if a breeze stirred the otherwise still night. Her skin was as pale as the face of a Titian angel. She smiled, and my heart caught. I saw my grandmother in her expression.

"Josie," she said.

I reached for her, but drew back my arm before it pierced the dome. Beata was a witch far more experienced than I, and her strength was glamour. She could too easily deceive me. I had to be on guard.

"I've been wanting to meet you for a long time," Beata said. She smiled, and warmth suffused me, tingling in my veins. "Thank you for summoning me."

This wasn't what I'd expected. I drew from the book at my feet and felt its energy course through me as if an umbilical cord attached us. As I focused on Beata, I caught a flash of Babe Hamilton—and someone else. Who?

"What do you want from me?" I asked.

"You've heard about me," Beata said.

"Yes. I've been warned." Behind me, Rodney growled. "You used your magic for selfish reasons. You stole your own sister's husband and drove him to suicide."

She dipped her head, then raised it. "Ailith," she said, naming my grandmother, her sister. After my nod, she continued. "I don't know exactly what she told you, but I'm certain there's one thing she left out."

I nudged my ankle an inch to feel Rodney's comforting weight. "Really?" I said, the doubt clear in my voice.

"My sister was a wonderful woman in many ways, but she was always jealous of me." She laughed once. "No. I would never seduce her husband." Beata's expression, calm and loving, confirmed it. "I did have a child out of wedlock, though. I'm assuming she told you about that. She didn't tell you who that child was, did she?"

What was she implying? I summoned the paltry amount of will I had left. "You set me up as a killer. I don't know how you did it, but somehow you made it look as if I was wandering town when Ian disappeared. You made Ian's body materialize in the atrium."

Wide-eyed, Beata shook her head. "I don't know what you're talking about. I would never do that. Why would I hurt you?" She drew her hands together, then opened them wide. "The murderer, the real one, must be framing you." She nodded slowly. "That's it. Someone is setting you up. Tell me more."

For a moment, I was confused. Of course it was Beata who'd framed me. Making me appear to be where I wasn't. Making notes vanish. Making bodies appear. No one but a witch could have pulled off this kind of deception.

"My grandmother warned me you'd find me, that you need me to break the spell holding back your full magic. Yet you want me in jail. Why is that?"

Beata glowed as if she were the good witch Glinda from *The Wizard of Oz*. A ring sparkled from her hand. Her dress—a gauzy linen shift—might have come from any era over the past few centuries. "Josie," she said, and the word was a caress. "Josie, you're family. You are closer to me than you could know. What you feel, I feel. Why do you think I've been watching you? To protect you. Let me help you."

She was so seductive. Conflict paralyzed me.

"It can be lonely being a witch. Perhaps you know that," Beata said.

Of course I understood that feeling of loneliness. I

had confessed to Sam that I was a witch. He couldn't handle it. My heart seized.

"You're family," Beata repeated. "Let me be here for you."

She reached forward as if to hug me, and I dropped my arms to my side. She couldn't breach the dome as long as I didn't pierce it first.

"Come now," she said in a soothing voice. "I don't want to hurt you. I want to help you."

"Help me?" Now my words came freely. "You've done the opposite for months. You stymied my power and cut off my magic by charming the linens you sold me. You sent crows to monitor me."

Beata's brows drew together. "I've what? No, you misunderstand. The crows were there to make sure you were okay. You're my family. More than that, you're. . . ."

A rustling beyond the trees drew both of our attention. A coyote? A bobcat, maybe? Then the woods were silent again. I couldn't get past the crazy feeling we were being watched. Nerves.

"What about the charmed quilt? Why did you do that?" I demanded.

She looked genuinely puzzled. "You thought I would hurt you? I intended to protect you. That's why I wove the glyph into it." Her expression relaxed. "My magic is still quite weak, and I might have miscalculated. I wanted you to feel cared for, not diminished."

When I didn't respond, she continued. "Think of the good things in your life these past months. You were almost killed not long ago."

She was right. I'd helped bring in a murderer, safely.

"Your time with Sam, the good times," she said. "Maybe I had something to do with protecting you. Did you think of that?" She stepped forward and raised a palm, but the protection dome held her back. She lowered her hand. "It's true that your grandmother— my sister—bound my magic. I was a powerful witch, like you. Now my magic is ordinary. There's only so much I can do to help you."

Aunt Beata was so convincing. She was loving, calm, and her energy melted into my wounded heart like honey in tea. Yet I knew the emotion I felt was my own need to be consoled, not her magic. Her magic couldn't trespass the dome.

Then again, wasn't that what glamour was—the ability to use your own needs and desires against you?

"I know you hurt," Beata said softly. "Sam let you down. Rejection like that—rejection of who you truly are—cuts deeply. I've seen how you've suffered. He ignored your calls and texts. He dismissed you like your time together meant nothing to him." She stepped closer. "You deserve better."

I was so tired. Her words tantalized me. This must be what an addict feels when she's been deprived of her drug of choice, then finds it dangled before her.

Again, something rustled in the brush, and my aunt's features seemed to harden—just for a second. I might have imagined it. Or had I?

"You're right. I need your help," I said. Tears burned at my eyes. "I don't know what's happening. I was so happy. Now my world is falling apart." I stooped to pick up *Grimm's Fairy Tales* and hugged it to my chest, feeling the soothing flow of magical energy.

"I understand."

I sank to sit on a rock. "I'm so in love with Sam. I know people can fall in and out of love, and that I could find someone else, but there's no one like Sam. No one."

It was true. I was hopelessly stuck on the way Sam looked at me when I spoke, as if the house could be on fire but my words were more important. I loved cooking dinner with him, Sam at the stove, me chopping herbs. I cherished our evenings on the back porch with Nicky playing and Sam telling me about his day as the sun set over the river. I even adored the crazy way Sam smiled when he was upset and frowned with happiness.

But he couldn't accept a fundamental part of who I was. A witch. I'd opened myself to him completely, and he'd turned his back without explanation. My heart ached more deeply than I ever thought possible. None of this would matter a whit, however, if I spent the rest of my life in prison.

Even if I were somehow cleared of the murder charge, my professional life was a shambles. The library's trustees openly fought about the children's books, and neither side seemed to value my opinion.

"I can help," Beata repeated. Her voice was warm, hypnotic, and flowed through my blood like whiskey. "You didn't deserve to be arrested. You didn't kill anyone," she said. By the thin light of my candle, Beata's resemblance to my grandmother grew. "You couldn't. Justice is in your blood. I understand."

I wanted to step forward and fall into her arms. The

past week had been the most difficult of my life, and the days to come didn't look to be any easier. Oh, how I craved comfort.

She let out a sigh. "Josie, how I wish you'd let me help you. If I had my full magic, I could. I could make it all go away." She spoke more rapidly. "I could find who murdered Tyrone Beaudrie and convince him to turn himself in."

"You're sure it's Tyrone?"

"Yes, Josie. It's him. I know."

"Who killed him?" I asked.

"I have an idea. Beaudrie has no doubt made a few enemies over the years. With my magic restored, I could extract a confession."

"With glamour," I said.

"Yes. It's my gift." Her eyes searched the dark sky. "I could make Sam see the truth about you, too, that you're a good, loving woman with the genetic anomaly of magic. He'd understand." She laughed, and the warmth lightened my heart. "I bet I could even get Wanda to love cats."

For a moment, I allowed myself to bask in the possibility. I'd be back in Sam's arms, inhaling his clean, woody scent and feeling the vibration of his voice in his chest. People in town would know I wasn't a criminal.

"If only my magic were released," Beata whispered, her gaze on mine.

That was it. My grandmother had been right. She wanted me to break my grandmother's containment spell.

I was the only person who could sever those bonds

for her. At the same time, she was the only person who could set me free, who could bring my old life back to me.

We stared at each other in the dark. Beata was serene, a faint smile on her face and a question in her eyes.

I stepped forward, through the protective dome, into her arms.

Chapter Twenty-seven

Aunt Beata's embrace was comforting, but there was something else. A feeling of sharp zaps, as if I were shorting out. I pulled back and searched her face. She smiled, sure and calm.

"Trust me, Josie."

Although the dome's protection was now shattered, Rodney continued to sit in its center, staring at us.

"What do you need?" I asked, knowing her response.

"One thing. Something simple. Then I can help you."

Anything. I'd do anything for relief. "Tell me."

"I need you to release my magic."

Of course it came to that. That's why Beata was here, why she'd sent crows to watch me. She was using the glamour she had at her disposal as an ordinary witch to lure me to do her bidding. I knew that. I wasn't that stupid.

But I also didn't care. I wanted my old life back, and she could do that for me.

I let my gaze sweep her, foot to head. She might have been a guardian angel from a nineteenth-century painting. Her eyes shone pale blue, and her resemblance to my grandmother gathered so that it was almost as if I were seeing her again. My heart squeezed in my chest. She could make my pain go away.

"Okay," I said.

At that simple word, the candle's flame grew brighter, taller, and burned purple. I opened *Grimm's Fairy Tales* at random to "Old Sultan," a tale that had always puzzled me, about the shifting alliances between a wolf and an elderly mutt. In it, the powerful wolf was deceived, thinking a three-legged cat's tail was a saber and its body a rock. The cat, in turn, believed a boar's ears to be a mouse and attacked them. I read aloud the words that glowed from the page:

"Listen to me, old fellow," said the wolf; "Be of good courage, I will help you in your need. I have thought of a way."

As the words left my lips, a deafening crack rent the night. The air around us thickened and swirled with magic so forceful that I struggled to not to drown in it. After a moment, my senses returned.

I watched Beata morph once again. The resemblance to my grandmother faded. Beata's face aged. She remained more beautiful than ever, but also more frightening. A sharp canniness replaced comfort and warmth. What had I done?

Then she laughed. Its force blew me back against a tree.

I heard a gasp. Was that me? "Beata?" The word sounded weak against the rage of power around us.

As a person, Beata remained on the small side—I was taller. As a witch, however, her magic made her a giant. She stretched her arms and swiveled her neck, as if relishing the energy that now flowed through them. This energy was not the strengthening flow I experienced, but something much darker, smelling of sulfur. It stung my eyes.

I'd made a monumental mistake.

"Goodbye, Josie."

Cold like a knife ripped through my gut. I'd just unleashed a terrible force. In the space of a moment, images of sobbing men, heartbroken women, dark rooms, and hollow hearts raced through my head. Rodney howled behind me.

Then Beata vanished.

I stood alone in the night. After the riot subsided, the woods became unnaturally quiet. And dark.

Blinded by pain, I had done something stupendously stupid. My grandmother had warned me Aunt Beata was not to be trusted, yet I'd trusted her. I'd wanted to believe her, and that was glamour's fuel. Turning anxiety to fear and fear to desperate acts, she'd made me believe what I wanted to believe. She'd amped up my pain, then used it against me. Beata was a master of mirroring people's desires. She could make herself into whatever someone wanted or needed, and I'd so desperately needed relief—relief from disasters she'd created.

Now I'd pay the price. I was in an even worse situation than when I'd started. I had no delusions that she'd clear me of Tyrone's murder or salvage my relationship with Sam. She'd used me and was done with me. All that talk about family and caring was just that: talk. I doubted I had the magic to rein her in again.

Worse, she might seek to lock me up for good so that I'd never have the chance to try to stem her magic. It would be child's play for her to finish the job and frame me for Tyrone's murder. As long as I was in prison, she'd be free to destroy lives wherever she landed. All along, her plan had been to make me need her, convince me to release her magic, then lock me away so I couldn't recapture it.

Twigs snapped, and I spun to see Lise Bloom step out from a copse of firs. Or was it? Wary, I held my breath. Lise had an unusual glimmer about her, an aura she hadn't shown before. Could this be Beata in another form?

However, unlike Beata, Lise walked unsurely and breathed unevenly. The air around her crackled.

"Josie?" she said at last, her voice wavering. "What just happened?"

Then I understood. This had happened to me almost two years ago. "Did you feel a big snap, like someone released a giant rubber band in your gut?"

Eyes wide, she nodded.

"You feel like you've lived under a veil your whole life until now?"

Again, a nod.

"You'll be all right."

Lise dropped to the log where Rodney had sat earlier. She rubbed her face and inhaled deeply. "Oh, my. Everything smells so . . . so rich. There's something else, too."

When I cast the spell to summon a witch, I must have drawn her as well as Beata. She hid while I talked with Beata. Lise was a witch. That's what I'd sensed in her. My spell releasing Beata's power had released hers, as well.

"What is it?" I asked.

"Worry, like leather and vinegar. And something much darker." She lifted her head and breathed deeply. "Can a person smell evil?" She looked straight at me. "What just happened between you and that lady?"

This was too much. I'd released the power of two witches, one with dark magic and one who had no clue what just happened. And I knew it was about to get much, much worse.

I looked at this newly minted witch, a woman whose magic was even greener than mine. Then I had an idea.

"Let's go back to the library," I said. "I have a lot to tell you."

Chapter Twenty-eight

L ise and I sat in Old Man Thurston's office. I didn't want to take her to my living room upstairs. Even with the curtains pulled shut, knowing Sam was sleeping just across the garden was too much to bear at that moment. My kitchen, although on the other side of the house, was cramped.

The office was cozy and dim, and I felt Old Man Thurston's hardworking energy here, even if he wouldn't recognize the room now. Someone, likely Mona, had turned face-out a handful of children's books featuring cats. The books murmured sleepily as I lit a candle. Electric lights would feel too harsh after the night's magical upheaval.

"Tell me," Lise said. "What happened back there?"

"Lise," I told her, "you're a witch."

If I was expecting shock or glee, I was disappointed. She sat calmly, as if she'd been waiting years for this explanation. "I see."

"Leo was right," I said. Rodney jumped on the desk

between us and offered his head to Lise to pet. "I'm a witch, too, but I'm relatively new to my magic. What you saw out there was me making a gigantic, horrendous mistake."

"You released the magic in someone else."

I nodded. "When I released her power, I must have released yours, too. She's my great aunt, and a powerful witch on her own. She's not a good person, though, and she uses her magic to ruin lives." Out of respect for my grandmother, I didn't go into details. "My grandmother cast a containment spell to limit her power. Unfortunately, I broke that spell."

And signed my own death warrant. I was under no illusions now. Beata would spend a few hours drunk with her new energy, but it wouldn't be long before she'd return to finish me off.

"How do you feel?" I asked. "This must all be overwhelming."

Lise nodded slowly, but she hadn't needed to tell me she was swimming in a world of questions and unusual sensations. Her intent yet distant stare said it all.

"It's like someone turned on the lights," she said, "when I hadn't even known I was living in the dark."

Boy, did that sound familiar. "How is it expressing itself? For me, it's about books. I've always loved reading, and the source of my magic is books."

The books sighed and washed me with energy when I mentioned them.

"It's smell," Lise said.

This was an odd one. "Smell? You mean, you smell things?"

Lise's brows drew together. "I think so. I think that's

it. I've always loved scent—not that I smell things like a bloodhound might, but I can parse smells."

Rodney leapt to my lap, and I absently dropped fingers to his back. He seemed unusually comfortable with Lise. "Tell me more."

"For instance, this house."

"Old wood and books," I said promptly.

"Yes, that for sure. Yesterday, I would have smelled how the heat lifted an almost bitter, leathery smell from the wood, and the books would have smelled like vanilla and must. But now"—her voice rose and expression became more animated—"it's really strange."

I didn't reply. She needed to figure this out on her own.

"It's like I'm smelling history." She rose and circled the room. "Here, for instance. I smell pipe tobacco."

As far as I knew, no one had smoked here for decades. She must be picking up on Old Man Thurston. "What else?"

"The sweet smell of children, like candy and milk." She touched *Puss in Boots*, proudly displayed cover out. "Duh, I guess you might say. We're in the children's section. But I smell something more." She stopped and turned to me. "Is it possible to smell emotion? I smell . . . frustration. Anger."

That would be Wanda. Part of the frustration was mine, for sure.

"More than that, though, I smell something tarry— something old and dark, on the verge of rotting." Her voice softened. "You're terrified."

The truth in Lise's assessment caused my stomach

to rise. I breathed slowly to calm it. "Yes. We'll get to that."

"Take your time," Lise said.

I had been so wrong to suspect Lise could be a facet of Beata. She held so much innocence. When I regained some of my composure, I said, "I discovered I was a witch only a few years ago, when I moved to Wilfred. Does the magic run through the women, like it does in mine?"

She dropped into her chair. "I don't know. I was adopted. That's why I'm here. I want to know where I came from."

Again, I let her talk. Tonight would be another long one. My body was exhausted, but my brain hummed with energy.

"I always knew there was something different about me. Not just different from my family—they're scientists—but different from regular people." Her words came faster as she let out thoughts she'd clearly harbored for years. I understood. "I felt like such a weirdo. An outsider. I've always been drawn to otherworldly things. Does that sound strange?"

"You're asking me?" I said.

"I've tried tracking down my biological family, but my adoption was . . . informal."

There was more to that story, I was sure, but I let her continue.

"I've sent my DNA a few times to one of the big companies, but something always went haywire. Once the results came back that I was one hundred percent Chinese. Another time they said I'd sent in the saliva of a squirrel." She sighed. "I took a summer job at a new age shop in Astoria, thinking I'd get some kind of insight on who I am." She frowned. "It didn't work, but I met Leo that way. When he mentioned you, I felt I had to see you. Maybe, somehow . . . you would understand me."

"I'm not an expert, and I haven't had a real life mentor, but I can tell you a few things about magic."

"I'm listening," she said.

"As far as I've been able to figure, witches each have an ability to tap into a particular energy. For instance, I love reading and adore books. This gives me the ability to tap into the energy authors and readers have poured into books—the plots, imagination, the hours they've spent with their eyes on the page and the stories coming to life in their minds. It's a massive power source."

She nodded. "I've always been sensitive to scent. When my parents had parties, I would bury my nose in the coats they tossed on the bed and smell the women's perfumes and the men's soap and the wool of their jackets. I swear I could even smell illness on some people's skins. But it's gone wild since then." She shook her head in bewilderment. "Now, as I said, it's like I can smell emotion."

"You mean, each emotion has a scent? How does that work?"

"You, for instance," Lise said. "Besides fear, I smell regret. It's a mixture of sadness and shame."

"What does it smell like?"

"Violets." She nodded. "Yes. You know how some flowers seem to give up their scent just before they die?

Like that. Violets in water that should have been changed days ago." Lise took a moment to digest her discoveries. "Out there in the woods. Beata. Could she be my mother—or yours? You heard her. Was she playing with you?"

"My grandmother told me Beata had a child who would be about our age. That's all I know." There was a sympathy between Lise and me, a vibe that could be explained by DNA—or simply by the fact that we both had unearthly abilities. "I wouldn't believe anything she said." I drew a deep breath. "But I wouldn't not believe it, either."

I'd unleashed Beata's full power, and Lise's. As the image of my aunt crossed my mind, the house's windows shook and walls whistled, as if a powerful wind had encircled the mansion. Eyes wide, Lise grabbed the edge of her chair. The books hummed in bass notes and whispered warnings, and a chill like a December ice storm dropped over us.

Beata would destroy lives now that her magic's potency had been restored. My throat tightened as I understood that my life would be the first. There was no way she'd let me go free. I had the power to release her magic, yes, but I also had the power to bind it again, and she knew it.

Lise sat back, her eyes closed, probably lost in the world of her own new abilities.

"Lise," I said, "I need you."

"I know."

Chapter Twenty-nine

I slept only five hours that night, but despite the whirlwind chaos of my thoughts, it was a hard sleep. The
book on my nightstand was more evidence I would
have to work fast: *The Perfect Storm*.

Beata would not rest until I was silenced. I wasn't
sure precisely what was up her sleeve, but I knew it
would have to do with pinning Tyrone's murder on me.
Which meant I had to find his killer first.

My first thought was that Beata was responsible for
Tyrone's death, but almost as quickly as I had the
thought, I dismissed it. Without her full magic, Beata
would have had to kill him the way a non-witch would,
and she wasn't physically strong enough to subdue
him. Besides that, Beata was an opportunist. My grandmother's letter had portrayed her as someone who
capitalized on the people and opportunities around
her—not someone who instigated them.

The books' contentment with having Lise among

them had morphed to simmering foreboding. Despite the sun flowing into each room as I pulled open the faded brocade curtains, the library's mood kept me on edge. Even Marilyn Wilfred seemed to telegraph alarm from her portrait above the atrium's entrance.

"Everything okay?" Roz didn't even lift her fingers from her keyboard as she talked, but she did toss a glance my way.

"So far," I said. "Want the ceiling vents lifted for a couple of hours?" After lunch, when the sun had traveled farther west, the conservatory would be flooded with sun and heat. Right now, the breeze off the river was cool.

Roz shut her laptop and turned to me. "What do you mean, 'so far'?"

"Just that." What else could I say? That my aunt, an evil witch to whom Roz had unknowingly rented her trailer, was on my tail? That the stranger wandering town had a magical sense of smell? That I was being framed for murder?

Her eyes narrowed, and she reached for her fan and flicked it open with the skills of a showgirl at the Moulin Rouge. "What's happening that I don't know?"

I shrugged.

"Are they going to throw you in the clink again?"

My shoulders dropped. "I hope not. Why?"

A moment passed, then two. Roz turned to her laptop. "Something is brewing around here, and I have a bad feeling about it. I'm not normally given to intuition, but I have the creeps, big time."

"Yes," was all I said.

"You're not out of woods on the murder rap. Then there's the follow-up trustees' meeting. Have you come up with a presentation?"

The trustees' meeting was the last thing on my mind. What good would it do if I was in jail? I hedged. "I'll get to it." I pulled up a chair. "You're plugged into the grapevine. Is there any word on who killed the man found in the woods?"

"You mean, besides you? Orson's taking odds at the tavern, and you're the favorite as the murderer, eight to one." She turned quickly again to her computer.

"Roz! You didn't. You put money on me, didn't you?"

She spoke, eyes on her keyboard. "I'm sure it was self-defense. Or a moment of passion. It's not like you're a natural born murderer. But look at the evidence: Sam dumps you, Tyrone makes up to you then hits on someone else. You've been seen going to the woods. You were looking for Tyrone the night he died. What are we supposed to think? All we need is your fingerprints on the murder weapon, and it's a done deal."

I'd thought I couldn't feel any worse. I was wrong. I was also certain Beata had already come to the same conclusion about the fingerprints. "Has the body been confirmed as Tyrone's?" I wouldn't take Beata's word.

"Dental records match up. Besides, who else could it be?" Roz said. "He's missing, a body shows up. Two and two make four."

Beata had been right. Poor Tyrone. He hadn't deserved this. "What else are they saying?"

"Speculation is that you're setting Ian up as the murderer. You're making a big deal about them being from the same town."

"You've got to be joking." Looking for Ian was what had gotten me into this whole mess. Emotion stormed in my chest like a hurricane, and I teetered on the edge of sobbing. Then, strangely, I burst into laughter. I laughed until my torso ached and tears dampened my cheeks. Roz stared at me without comprehension.

"What's so funny?" Sam stood in the conservatory's doorway. My breath stuck in my throat. I'd always found him handsome, but today his early receding hairline and intent gaze pitched even more longing into my heart. Had I told him how much I loved him when I'd had the chance? Did he know the hundred ways I appreciated him: his cooking skills, his focused listening, his gentleness with Nicky, his firm sense of right and wrong?

"I just—Roz thinks. . . ." As quickly as laughter had consumed me, now seeing Sam's distant expression, I wanted to cry. "Can I help you?"

He lifted a clear zip-top bag with something thin and stained red coiled inside. "I found this in the brush out back, on the slope to the river."

My heart dropped. I had a hunch I knew exactly what it was and what it meant for me. I squeezed my eyes shut.

"What is it?" Roz asked, saving me the trouble.

"A zip tie, the long type found on construction sites. Almost certainly used to strangle Tyrone Beaudrie." He lowered his arm. My eyes, now open, followed the bag.

"The murder weapon," I said. So that was how Beata was going to do it. That's how she'd make sure I was locked away for good.

"I'm sending it to the lab right now." Sam's expression was impossible to read, despite the hours I'd spent gazing at it over the past months. "Josie, by tomorrow morning, I'll have a search warrant."

I had to find Tyrone's murderer, and I had to find him now. I opened my mouth to tell Roz I needed to leave, but she beat me to it.

"You go," she said. "I'll take care of the library."

Roz might have expected me to trudge upstairs to pull a quilt over my head and weep. Instead I made my way for the kitchen door and strode down the hill to town. Sam's SUV was already gone, the zip tie with him. Every minute counted.

I took a left into the Magnolia Rolling Estates. Breathless, I knocked on Ian's door. *Please let him be home*, I prayed.

Lalena, her expression stern, appeared behind the screen. "What do you want?"

For a moment, I was taken aback. Then I remembered my conversation with Roz. "You think I murdered Tyrone Beaudrie and am trying to pin it on Ian."

"I don't think you murdered anyone." She looked at her feet. "You wouldn't do that. But at the café, they're saying you're the prime suspect, and you're looking for somewhere to cast the blame."

She looked wary but didn't close the door. I took

that as encouragement. "I'm not trying to pin anything on Ian. Please. I need to see him."

"Let her in," Ian said. He'd rolled up behind Lalena.

Lalena reluctantly stepped aside.

"Thank you," I said. "I need to find out who killed Tyrone. Someone is setting me up for it."

"Have a seat," Ian said. "Slow down, and tell us what's on your mind."

Lalena remained silent.

I looked at them both, then took the couch. Lalena would come around eventually. "Sam found a zip tie in the bushes, and he thinks it's what was used to kill Tyrone. It's at the crime lab by now. The thing is. . . ."

"The thing is what?" Ian prompted.

I hated to say it. "The thing is, I think they'll find my fingerprints on it. Or something that will incriminate me." How Beata would pull it off, I didn't know, but I knew she'd pull it off somehow. Perhaps she'd collected one of my hairs. Or—the cup of coffee she'd made me when she'd given me the sheet with my initials and the glyph. She might have lifted my fingerprints from the mug.

"What makes you so sure?" Lalena asked.

There was no way I could explain it that they would understand. "I'm asking you to believe me."

Lalena looked at Ian. "Why should I?"

"Lalena, you know me. Am I that sort of person?"

She glanced at the carpet, then disappeared down the hall. When she returned, she held a deck of tarot cards. She closed her eyes and pulled one. Whatever she saw on the card relieved her. "The priestess. Either you're telling the truth or you're a witch." She laughed. "Or both."

"Ha ha," I said. If she only knew. "I thought you didn't believe in tarot cards."

"It was a tiebreaker," she replied.

"You think we can help," Ian said. "How?"

I shook my head. "Maybe Tyrone's—Byron, as you know him—death is related to his, um"—I glanced at Lalena—"work in Baltimore."

"She knows," Ian said. "I explained why I had to leave." Lalena looped an arm around his shoulders. "Go on."

"He was some kind of criminal kingpin. Surely he had enemies," I said. "Maybe one of them followed him here. Maybe it's someone you'd recognize."

"It's possible," Ian said. "Byron was a bad dude. Really twisted. I don't know anyone, though, who'd be stupid enough to track him down. Once he was out of their life, they'd leave him be. I know I would."

A car crunched up the gravel drive that formed the spine of the Magnolia Rolling Estates. Lalena got up to look out the window. "It's the sheriff's office. They're going to my house." She dropped the curtain and swiveled to face me. "I bet they're looking for you, Josie."

That was fast. My heart froze in my chest. The noose was tightening. Somewhere, Beata was laughing.

"They'll stop here next," Ian said.

Lalena's eyes widened. "Josie, hide."

Chapter Thirty

Ian gestured down the hall. "First door on the left." Ian's second bedroom was kept as an office. The room held a table and stacks of boxes ready to be taped together and sent full of books to customers.

I slipped open the closet doors and flattened myself against a wall, closing the doors after me. I slowly slid to the floor and drew my knees to my chest. All around me, Ian's stock of books murmured words of comfort, but my pulse beat faster than Wanda's flamenco records.

Truth will prevail, one book whispered. Its author had liked clichés. I hoped this one was true.

Live out your life in truth and justice, quoted a work by Marcus Aurelius.

The doorbell rang. A sheriff's deputy was here.

Outside of the books' encouragement, I couldn't hear much. My side touched the trailer's outer wall, and snatches of conversation reached me. Sounds of sniffing—Sailor—came from just outside the door. He let out a friendly bark.

"Hush, Sailor," I whispered, eliciting another playful yip. This was not time to play.

"Sailor," Lalena shouted from the other room, "stop barking at your toy. I'll get it out in a moment."

His collar jangled as he left the guest room. I dropped my jaw to breathe more quietly through my mouth, and although my knees ached in my crouched position, I didn't dare move.

After a few minutes, the front door closed. Then came the sound of a car starting up—presumably the deputy, leaving. Still, no one came to release me. I silently praised Ian's and Lalena's prudence.

At last, Lalena slid open the closet door. "All clear, but stay away from the windows."

"What did they say?" I bent to stretch my achy back and legs, then followed Lalena to the living room, where I sat well away from view.

"It wasn't Sam—it was some other deputy, looking for you. She didn't say much. When I suggested you'd be at the library, she said Sam was up there now."

Soon he'd be searching my apartment. I remembered the underwear and bras hanging to dry in my bathroom. That was the least of my problems.

"In other words, if I'm spotted, I'll be arrested for murder."

No one spoke. They didn't need to.

"We'll help you, won't we, Ian?" Lalena said.

"What can we do?" Ian said.

"Someone killed Tyrone," I said. "Meanwhile, the

sheriff's office is focused on finding evidence to support their theory that I strangled Tyrone with a zip tie." The thought nauseated me, and I flattened a palm to my stomach. "It's up to me to find the real murderer. If it had to do with his business dealings in Baltimore, you're my only hope."

He wheeled back a few inches. "I've told you everything I know."

"Could Josie be right and there's someone else here from your old gang?" Lalena asked Ian.

"It's all we have to go on."

"Why would they come out here?" Ian said.

"Why did Tyrone come out here?" I countered.

"To escape someone or something," Lalena said.

"Exactly," I said. "Maybe he brought a colleague."

"There's no one new in town who's not part of the construction operation," Ian pointed out. "No one I've seen, anyway."

This was true. Wilfred was small enough that we made a note when a new UPS driver stopped by.

"Except the woman at the retreat center. Lise," Lalena said.

"She's okay," I said quickly. "And Tyrone is dead, so you're safe from him. Would you be willing to go to the Empress and see if you recognize anyone else from Baltimore? It's a thin lead, but it's all I have to go on."

Ian looked into his lap.

"If you're right," I added, "you won't see anyone you know. It's perfectly safe."

Now Ian met my gaze. "If I'm not right? I don't

want to run into anyone from my old life. Even if it's not Byron, it's a world I don't want to stir up again."

I understood Ian's hesitation. But what else could I do? It wouldn't be long before the sheriff's office would catch up with me, and I had no idea what other tricks Beata might have up her sleeve.

I drew an audible breath. "If you see one of them, we might have found a murderer."

We were silent. Ian fidgeted with the arm of his wheelchair; I held Sailor in my lap; Lalena paced the living room. I was helpless unless Ian agreed to check out the construction site.

Finally, Lalena took charge. "This is what we'll do. Ian, you'll go to the Empress and pretend you want to talk to Orson about books in the new brewpub. It would be nice to have a shelf of novels customers could read while they kick back with a beer."

"Books on parapsychology?" I asked. I imagined customers sampling IPAs while they learned about Victorian ghost photography.

"He can find other books," she said. "Josie, you'll stay here. Ian can tell us if he sees anyone he knows."

"I need to go, too." Whoever Ian recognized, I wanted to see firsthand. If Aunt Beata had anything to do with it, maybe I'd sense her energy. Forewarned was forearmed.

Lalena shook her head. "No. It's too risky. In exactly two seconds, someone will report you to the sheriff's office."

"I've got to go along," I said. "This is my mess to sort out, not yours."

The tension was high among us, except for Sailor, who panted at Lalena's feet with a rubber hot dog in his mouth.

Lalena caved first. "Okay, but you're going in disguise." She smiled, slowly, until she nearly glowed. "Hang on. I'll be back in a minute." With Sailor at her feet, she crossed the lane to her home.

I took advantage of the few minutes alone with Ian. "What are you not telling me?"

"You know everything I know," he said.

"You're clearly afraid. Tyrone is gone. What's eating you?"

He tapped the wheel of his chair as he considered his words. "It's hard to explain, more a feeling than anything. I should be safe. Byron—Tyrone, as you know him—is dead. But I don't feel safe."

I understood "feelings" like this.

The door burst open, and Lalena arrived with an armload of clothing. "This is what we're going to do," she said. "Josie, you're Ian's mom."

"My mother's dead," Ian said.

"Honey, I'm sorry." Lalena kissed him on the cheek. There was still so much they didn't know about each other. "Today, Josie will be your mom. She's come to see you because you're planning to marry me, and she wants to check me out."

Ian shot her an inquiring glance. "We're getting married, huh?"

"That's the story." Lalena gave Ian a stern look. "It also explains why you've been gone. You took a few days with her in Portland. Now you're showing her Wilfred. I'll come, too." She plunked a box of hair dye on the table. "Let's get started."

Chapter Thirty-one

An hour later, I had streaky black hair—the sheer volume and fluff of my hair made complete coverage impossible—and wore a 1990s pink velour tracksuit left in Lalena's trailer by its former owner, her aunt, a devotee of pink.

I stuffed the last of a peanut butter and jelly sandwich into my mouth and asked, "What about my face? People will recognize me."

Lalena waved a pair of gold-rimmed sunglasses with lenses shaped like large butterflies. "This. And lipstick." With her other hand, she produced a tube. "Snowdrift peony." She uncapped it. Pink frost, naturally. "Ready?"

I felt like an extra in a 1990s sitcom. The only thing worse than life imprisonment would be life imprisonment with a bad dye job.

"My mother is rolling in her grave," Ian said. "She was an attractive woman."

"Thanks a lot," I said.

"Your mother is fine," Lalena told Ian. "What? You don't believe me? I'm a career medium, remember?"

Ian unlocked the door. "Come on. Let's get this over with."

I stood. How I hoped we'd find something, anything, to point toward Tyrone's killer.

"One last detail." Lalena slipped a diamond solitaire onto her ring finger and kissed Ian's cheek. "My grandmother's. Thank you, honey."

For a man ambushed by a spur-of-the-moment engagement, he took it well. "Excelsior!"

Leaving Ian's place felt like jumping from an airplane, unsure of the parachute's rip cord. I feared someone would recognize me. Partway down the Magnolia Estates' drive, though, I started to relax. My disguise was pretty good. Maybe it would be okay, after all.

Outside the café, we encountered our first obstacle, in the form of Patty. Her gaze fastened on me with the urgency of a bird dog in duck territory. "What's this?" she asked.

I froze. The sunglasses obscured the top half of my face. My hair had been twisted into a tight bun, and I'd surely wiped most of the errant hair dye from my face. Hadn't I?

Patty stepped closer, her eyes narrowing. "Is that?" Another step. "Is that tracksuit Juicy Couture?"

I relaxed in relief. Of course. Patty was obsessed with the exercise culture of thirty-plus years ago. She still mourned the disappearance of leg warmers and step aerobics video tapes.

Before I could formulate a fake voice in which to reply, Lalena stepped in. "I'd like you meet Ian's

mother"—her gaze wandered the parking lot—
"Escalade."

I nearly choked. *Escalade?* I supposed it could be
worse. Next to the showy Escalade sat a Bronco.

Patty's eagle eye was distracted by Lalena's ring,
winking in the afternoon sun. "Oh my, you and Ian . . . ?"

"We're getting married!" Lalena said. "I'm showing
Mama Escalade around town. We get along great." She
beamed. "I feel like we're already best friends."

I smiled like a proud mother-in-law to be.

"No time to chat now!" Lalena grabbed my arm.
"Come on, Mom. You'll love what they're doing to our
old movie theater." I waved to Patty, who had changed
course to return to the café to spread the news.

"You're going to have to have a good story after this
for why the wedding isn't coming off," I said under my
breath.

"Who said it isn't?" Lalena said. Ian remained
silent, but he smiled.

At the Empress, two workers were on scaffolding,
prying up strips of siding. I glanced at Ian, who paused
on the sidewalk to examine the men. He gave me a subtle shake of the head.

Orson ambled over, a mug of coffee in hand. "Nice,
eh?" He winked at me and stuck out his free hand.
"Don't believe I've met you. I'm Orson, owner of the
soon-to-be Empress Brewpub."

I didn't want to speak, and it turned out I didn't have
to. Lalena was enjoying herself. "This is Ian's mom,
Escalade. We've told her so much about the Empress.
Could we go inside and have a peek? Ian wants to talk
to you about books for the brewpub, too."

Orson's eyes were glued on me. "I'd love to show you and the little lady around, but it's a work site. Dangerous."

If only he knew how dangerous it might be. I forced what I hoped was a smile of appeal.

"Please?" Lalena asked. "I'm sure you have extra hard hats."

Ian finally spoke. "Mom loves a good construction site."

Orson relented, giving us hard hats from a stack near the door and pointing out the ramp Ian could use where wheelbarrows of construction materials went in and out. He looked at his phone. "I have to take this call. Ian, we can talk books later. See you soon, I hope, Escalade."

Inside, the Empress was cooler and smelled of sawdust and damp plaster. I'd been here over the spring, before Orson conceived his plan of converting the theater. Then it had been a time capsule of the 1970s, complete with moldy movie posters and rotting popcorn still in the snack bar. Today the theater was busy with workers. The ticket booth still stood, but the grand light fixtures were shrouded and walls open to the studs. The carpets had been ripped out, and a stack of lumber occupied much of the lobby.

Again, I glanced at Ian. He surveyed the half dozen workers toting materials here and there, and again he shook his head.

We advanced to the theater's heart, the former viewing room. Here I knew most of the work would be taking place. The seats would need ripped out, for one, and the floor leveled. Orson had told us the brewing equipment would be on the stage, and the seating area would become a dining room and bar.

The viewing room hummed with activity. A stack of Sheetrock was being wheeled in with a forklift, and a framing crew worked on one side of the room. Ian was challenged to wheel his chair around the chaos. All told, perhaps a dozen people wielded saws and nail guns, or moved materials. Ian scanned them but showed no sign of recognition.

It was a bust. With no connection to Ian's old world, I had nothing to go on. No potential murderer, which left me as the prime suspect. How long would it be before someone recognized me? I couldn't hide out forever.

"Let's go," I said. Before I turned for the door, I halted. There, stacked on piping, was a bundle of zip ties exactly like the one Sam said had killed Tyrone.

My head ached. Maybe I should turn myself in now. Maybe it would make my sentence lighter. Did I have any hope of getting out of this?

Outside, the sun felt doubly strong. Someone would recognize me. I stood out too much not to draw attention in a small town like Wilfred.

Ian's chair rolled to a stop. "Over there," he said under his breath. His face had gone white. "You told me he was dead."

Cliff Montgomery emerged from a dusty panel van in the vacant lot next to the Empress. He tugged from a can of Red Bull and squinted against the sun.

"The framer?" I asked.

"That's him. That's Byron."

Chapter Thirty-two

Back at Ian's trailer, I ripped the sunglasses from my face. "Get your laptop," I told him.

It had been torture to pretend to stroll nonchalantly back to the Magnolia Rolling Estates when all I'd wanted to do was race to a computer and log into the library's periodicals database to search Byron's name. Both he and Tyrone had come to Wilfred for a reason. Either they'd sought Wilfred specifically or, more likely, were on the run from somewhere else.

"He's here," Ian said, unable to hide sheer panic. "I should have never come back. We need to leave. Lalena, you're not safe, either."

"The sooner he's in jail," Lalena said, "the sooner we're all safe. Especially Josie."

She was a good friend. If I survived the next few days, I'd make sure the library's bathtub was always stocked with high-end bubble bath.

"I feel like an idiot for believing Tyrone was Byron,"

I said. "Obviously Tyrone was his name, or the medical examiner wouldn't have been able to make an I.D."

"Don't worry about it. We know now." Lalena drew the curtains as I called up the database and typed in Byron's name. I scored right away—an article from the *Baltimore Sun*:

> Tyrone Beaudrie and Byron Marshall sought for questioning in a homicide. The two men were seen leaving Marvin's TV and Appliance Tuesday night at approximately 11:30 p.m. Proprietor Marvin Chang was found dead of a gunshot wound when employees arrived the next morning.

Honey," Lalena said, her arm on Ian's shoulder. The engagement ring still sparkled from her finger. "Don't worry. I've got your back."

"Did you know Tyrone?" I asked.

"No. Never heard of him." He shook his head in amazement. "I'm not surprised about Byron, though."

"This explains why they left town." I closed the laptop. "Although it doesn't explain why Byron would have killed Tyrone."

"The murder might not have been planned," Ian said. "Maybe this guy Tyrone wanted to turn himself in, and Byron wouldn't stand for it."

"Maybe Byron pulled the trigger," Lalena pointed out. "He would have had more to lose."

Now I saw my conversations with Tyrone in a completely different light. "I'd buy that. When I talked to him, Tyrone seemed to be intent on changing his life. Maybe Cliff—excuse me, Byron—didn't share those views."

"It could have been anything," Ian said. "I tell you, Byron is a dangerous man. Once I saw him break a man's finger on a bet." He made a snapping motion with his hands and flinched at the memory.

"It's not enough to go on," I said. "The police would be very interested to know Byron is here, but that won't prove he killed Tyrone. It won't clear my name." I drummed my fingers on the kitchen table. "As far as we know, Byron, calling himself Cliff, has no idea anyone has caught onto who he really is."

"We should delay telling the sheriff. Is that what you're getting at?" Ian said.

"It wouldn't be for long," I said. It couldn't be. Between the hunt for me and Aunt Beata's magical efforts, every minute that ticked by worked against me. "How can I prove he killed Tyrone, that I didn't do it?"

"You mean, *we* prove. You're not doing this alone," Lalena said.

My heart warmed, and I wanted to cry. "Thank you."

Ian dropped a hand to pet Sailor's head, but it was clear his mind was somewhere else. "If Byron found out I was here. . . ." He shook his head. "I don't want to think about it."

There were two of us in hiding now. Me from the sheriff, and Ian from Byron. We all stared sullenly at random spots in the room.

I let out a long breath. "Let's walk through the night Tyrone died. Maybe there's something we're overlooking, something that could nail Cliff. I mean, Byron."

"Something the sheriff's department missed?" Lalena said. "What makes us better than they are? They have labs and whole teams of specialists."

"We know about Byron, and they don't. Besides, they think they have their suspect." I didn't need to add "me."

"Okay. I'm listening," Ian said. "I'm happy to brainstorm ideas, and I want Byron locked up. I can't risk him knowing I'm here."

"Hang on a minute," Lalena said. She plugged in the window unit air conditioner. "So no one overhears us."

I caught a glimpse of myself in the reflection from the window and flinched at my hair and pink velour get-up. I moved to the couch and drew up my legs. "Tyrone died sometime the night before last. How did it go down?"

Ian turned his chair to face me, and Lalena took the opposite end of the couch. Ian spoke first. "Tyrone was found in the woods. It seems unlikely that Byron killed Tyrone in town and dragged his body up the hill and into the forest. He must have met him somewhere, and they walked there together."

I nodded. "I saw Byron on the trail a few days ago. He might have been scoping a place to hide Tyrone's body." A grisly thought. I gulped from my glass of water. "But back to that night. Tyrone had left the guest house early that evening. I know, because I'd received a note to meet him. I looked for him at the guest house and the café, but he wasn't there." The note had disappeared. Undoubtedly Beata's work. The note may not have even been from Tyrone in the first place, but a trick so I'd be seen asking around for him.

Lalena picked up the thread. "Byron took him to the woods and strangled him with a zip tie."

"How did you know that?" I asked. I'd seen Sam with the zip tie, but I hadn't known it was conclusively the murder weapon.

"Marjorie at the sheriff's office gets her hair done by Candace, who passed it on to Patty, who told me at the café this morning."

Good grief, there were no secrets in this town. "You'd think with this kind of intelligence, the murderer would have been caught practically before he struck."

Lalena continued. "They found keys, but no wallet on the body. That's why they assumed the dead man was Ian. They didn't have a reason to think otherwise." She rose and pecked him on the cheek before returning to the sofa.

"Byron would never be so stupid as to keep Tyrone's wallet. You can bet he burnt it, minus the cash," Ian said.

A thought began to crystallize. "What keys did they find?"

"A key ring, I think she said."

I remembered the key hooks near the Wallingford Guest House's front door. Each key hung on a brass tag. "Was the guest house key found?"

"Patty didn't mention it."

"Tyrone would have had it on his body somewhere. Maybe it's still out there," I said.

"You mean, maybe Byron has it," Ian said. "That's an idea."

"He wouldn't know he still has the key, of course," I said. "He might simply have overlooked it."

Lalena reached for her phone and tapped out a text. Almost instantly, her phone chimed in reply. "Patty doesn't know. She's texting Candace."

The next minutes stretched on. My hope alternately grew and was crushed as I ran through scenarios in my mind. If Byron had overlooked the guest house key and kept it, it might provide the evidence the sheriff needed to arrest him. People overlooked details, especially people under a lot of stress. Byron had easy access to the zip ties at the Empress, and Tyrone would have trusted him enough to follow him into the woods.

On the other hand, my future as a free person rested on a slender piece of metal. If Byron was smart enough to destroy anything linking Tyrone to the body in the woods, he surely would have tossed the key into the river.

Lalena's phone chimed again. Ian and I watched her as if she were reading the results of a blood test for a possibly terminal case.

"Patty says Candace says Marjorie says 'No.' No guest house key."

I had a chance after all. I rose and grabbed the butterfly-lensed sunglasses.

"Where are you going?" Lalena asked.

"To get that key. Or at least to see if Byron has it. If he does, we'll know for certain he killed Tyrone."

"No, you don't," Ian said. "You can't just charge out of here and ask Byron if he happens to have a dead man's room key, or you'll be his next victim. Guaranteed."

"If she doesn't get picked up by the sheriff first," Lalena added.

"If Byron has the key, he doesn't know it," I said. "If he has it—"

"A big *if*," Ian said.

"—it's in his van, likely in the pocket of whatever he wore that night." There would have been no reason to destroy his clothes. Any scraps left from burning them might be traced to him.

"You're going to break into his van and search for the key?" Lalena stood, her voice incredulous. "That's nuts. Besides, what if you do find it? The sheriff will think you had the key all along and that you planted it on Byron. You definitely don't want your fingerprints on it."

I had plans for that key. If the key existed, that was. I needed it for more than clearing my name with the sheriff's office. This would be the biggest test of my magic yet.

"True," I said. "This is not your problem—it's mine. You two have done enough to help, and I can't tell you how grateful I am."

"Josie, don't be foolish. You don't know Byron like I do. You read the article. He won't hesitate to kill you."

Lalena's eyes were wide. "I know you're desperate, but don't put yourself at risk. Look at what happened to Ian."

Ian rolled back a few inches. "To me?"

"The injury, your scar," she said. "Byron is ruthless."

"This?" Ian gestured toward his legs. "I got injured falling off the bleachers at a concert. What did you think happened?"

Lalena hugged him. "Never mind. We can talk about it later. Bottom line, it would still be stupid for Josie to look for the room key."

I looked from Ian to Lalena. They were both right, of course. I could call the sheriff's office, turn myself in, and tip them off about Byron. Over the course of a few days, they might come to the same conclusion we had. Or not.

However, in the meantime, Beata would orchestrate whatever final details she needed to ensure I was the one behind bars. She had already woven a veil of glamour around the murder that turned heads toward me as Tyrone's killer. If she planted the room key at the library, I was as good as convicted.

Once I was out of the picture, she would go on to destroy whomever stood between her and whatever glory she sought, whenever she wanted it. The damage she'd done as a young woman was nothing compared to the ruin she could wreak now. My sense of justice would not allow it.

I had no choice. "I'm not going to get the key, Escalade is."

That was a lie. This job was all Rodney's.

Chapter Thirty-three

I took the long way to the Empress. Butterfly sunglasses in place, streaky black hair fastened under a pink baseball cap, I walked through the back of the trailer park and around the café through the meadow. I furtively crossed Wilfred's main drag and tried my best to look like a visiting East Coaster named Escalade, fascinated by small-town Oregon ways. Then I darted to the Empress and crouched behind a dumpster. I leaned against its hot steel side and caught my breath.

All this time, Rodney was at my feet. He never failed to sense when magic was in the offing. I still had no idea where he'd come from originally, only that he'd shown up at the library shortly before I'd arrived in Wilfred, as if he were waiting for me. We'd firmly bonded, and I couldn't imagine life without him.

"Are you ready for your assignment, buddy?" I asked him.

As usual, he looked as if he wasn't paying attention. He nonchalantly groomed his hindquarters, the sun glistening on his blue-black fur. He'd heard me, all right.

A dozen or so trucks filled the vacant lot next to the Empress. Byron's van was on the lot's far edge, away from the street. The driver's side window was partially open, giving Rodney an entrance. However, I needed to be near him to maintain our connection.

At the sound of boots on gravel, I drew in my knees and kept still. The sides of the dumpster clanged, making me jump and sending Rodney under it as wood debris hit its metal sides. The steps receded, and I regained my breath. Yet another reason I'd need to move.

I poked my head around the dumpster. Rodney G.I. Joed his way out next to me. The coast was clear. Keeping low, I hustled across the lot and slid under Byron's van. Near my hip was a fast-food wrapper and a Red Bull can teeming with ants. It was cooler here, at least, even if it smelled of motor oil. Rodney purred at my shoulder.

Rodney, I willed him, *go into the van*. I pictured Rodney jumping from gravel to the van's step and scuttling through the window. *Look for the key*. Again I formed a picture, this time of a room key with its brass tag from the Wallingford Guest House. *Got it?*

In response, Rodney crawled from under the van. He easily bounded to the driver's side step with its rubber mat, then up to the window, his claws catching the window's edge. I breathed deeply and let my mind relax. Now I was in Rodney's head, seeing through his eyes.

Good grief, the van was a mess. Byron might have organized an efficient criminal enterprise in Baltimore, but he was no housekeeper. From the sight of the wadded sleeping bag and tangled workpants, he'd been living here. A few soda cans rattled in the foot well. Despite the clutter, the van's energy was thin. No books.

Start looking, Rodney, I urged him. The key.

Someone could come by anytime. Lunch was over, but didn't construction workers generally start and stop work early?

Through Rodney's eyes, I surveyed the van's edges. He made a circuit of the back, padding over dirty socks and a foam pad used as a mattress. He stuck his nose in a half-opened Dopp bag. Nothing there but a razor, toothbrush, and, strangely, a set of gold cufflinks with horses' heads on them. Their eyes twinkled with diamonds. No key.

The pants, I told Rodney. Check the pockets.

For a moment, my attention came back to myself under the van. I scratched an ankle with my foot to dislodge an ant. *Focus*, I told myself and drew a breath, taking me back to Rodney.

A wadded pair of Carhartts protruded from under the sleeping bag. With his teeth, Rodney pulled them farther out until the top pockets were within easy reach. He stuck a paw in one pocket and dug around. From Rodney's body I felt a penny and a gum wrapper.

The other pocket. Rodney walked over the pants and clawed them to the side for easier access. This pocket was completely empty. However, partway down the leg was yet another pocket.

Try it, I urged Rodney.

He clawed the pants free of the sleeping bag, and

from the tiny weight moving with the pants leg, it was immediately apparent something was there. Rodney dove his whole head into the dark pocket and pulled it out. The key to Tyrone's room at the Wallingford Guest House.

This was it! The proof. Byron really had killed Tyrone. From under the van, I was dizzy. Whether it was from the magic I'd expended or from the heat and my cramped position, I wasn't sure. What I was sure of, though, was that as soon as Byron changed his pants, he'd realize he still had the key, and he'd almost certainly destroy it.

Should I take the key? I couldn't. If I brought it to Sam, he would only see it as proof that I'd killed Tyrone, that I was trying to frame Byron. Otherwise, how would I have the key at all? It would do my reputation no good if I let on that I broke into Byron's van to find it. No. I now had proof of Byron's guilt. I'd leave the evidence. But not where he could find it.

Hide the key, I willed Rodney.

I felt Rodney resist. Worse, he was backing away from the key. Through his eyes I saw its brass tag catch the light on the floor of the van.

Something was wrong. I let my mind relax into Rodney's body. Then I felt it. Magic shrouded the key, bad magic. Beata's magic. She was on to the key's existence—perhaps had known of it all along—and no doubt planned to use it as the final piece of evidence to frame me as Tyrone's killer.

Anger surged through me. Rodney yowled.

I clenched my fists and released them. I didn't have

the luxury of flipping out. Not now. Again, I took hold of my breath. After a moment, I formed the words.

Rodney. I was firm and calm. *You must take the key and hide it.* I scanned the van. *Under the passenger seat.*

He refused to move. I understood. The key burned and would taste of sulfur in his mouth.

Come on, guy, I urged. *We need to do this.*

So suddenly that I startled, Rodney leapt forward and grasped the key. I felt nausea rise as the key scorched his tongue with the taste of rotten eggs. He bolted to the passenger seat and dropped it, then backed away, his head thrusting forward with the effort of not vomiting.

Keep going, I told him. *We can do this.*

He extended a paw and ripped a hole in the bottom of the upholstery. He growled as he shoved the key into the hole.

My head fell back against the gravel. *Good boy,* I told him. *You can come out now. We're safe.*

Footsteps, a few sets, sounded across the lot. I'd spoken too soon.

"See you tonight at the tavern?" a voice called, getting closer.

Above me, the van door creaked open. It was Byron.

I was firmly back in my body, but I sensed Rodney all the same. He'd scurried to the back of the van and tried to blend in with the wadded sleeping bag.

Then the van's engine started up. I swore under my breath. It wouldn't matter if I avoided prison if I ended up dead from being run over. My magic was useless here, with no books to feed it. I screwed my eyes shut and waited for the worst.

The engine cut. "Get out! You hear me?"

The driver's side door opened, and Rodney, growling, hit the gravel and took off.

I rolled out on the opposite side and ran as if my life depended on it. In fact, it did.

Chapter Thirty-four

Fear fueled my escape from the Empress's parking lot, across the old highway, and up through the trailer park, where Rodney darted from the rosebushes surrounding Lalena's palm reading sign to join me. I'm sure I drew attention, but I'd leave Lalena and Ian to explain why Ian's mother had shot off on a spontaneous trail run.

Midway across the meadow, I collapsed on my back to catch my breath and let my adrenaline settle. The knee-high grass hid me. I stared into the blue sky, the sun beating down, and filled my lungs with fresh air to cleanse them of the stale odor of Byron's van and the trash-strewn gravel under it. It was peaceful here, and I was safe—for the moment. Right now, Sam and the homicide detectives would be combing Wilfred, looking for me.

I was almost certain I knew Aunt Beata's next steps. Getting the guest house key would be no problem for her, thanks to the glamour I'd stupidly, perhaps fatally, unleashed. She could appear as the exact seductress Byron/Cliff sought. He'd open his van to her and, with a smile, watch her search it. She was going to plant the key at the library for Sam to find when he showed up tomorrow, search warrant in hand. It would be the final step in her plan to lock me up where I couldn't rein in her magic.

Rodney trotted through the grass and curled up, purring, in my armpit. His black fur was warm with sun.

What now?

Beata was a powerful witch. So was I, but did I have the experience to subdue her? If only I could get to my grandmother's grimoire. Perhaps there was something in it—anything—that could help me rebind Beata's magic.

I sat up. The meadow's dry grass rustled in the slight breeze, and grasshoppers hummed. A cooler waft of air smelling of damp stone drifted from the millpond. Alone, Beata's power might be too much to handle. But I wasn't alone.

"Come on, Rodney." Checking to make sure no one was within sight, I made my way toward the woods. The forest was quiet, and I saw no one on the trail, but Sam knew I used it to travel between the library and re-treat center. He could be here anytime to look for me. I ducked off the trail to take the overgrown spur to the witch's circle.

The witch's circle was cool, even in the heat of the summer afternoon. Tall firs ranged thickly above. I leaned against the rugged bark of a strong old tree and closed my eyes.

How could I draw Lise to me? I didn't have her phone

number, and I didn't have a book to draw magic from to fuel a spell. However, we were both witches, bound by centuries of shared experience, even if she was just beginning to be aware of it.

Her power came from scent. That's where I'd start.

I closed my eyes and inhaled. Rodney's purrs kicked up a notch. The fir trees breathed a damp, piney aroma, almost like incense. Below me, the balsamic fragrance of dried needles was tinged with hay. Charcoal and the lingering rose and sandalwood of magic drifted from where I'd burned Beata's linens—and where Tyrone's body had been found. *Lise, come*, I willed.

I let out my breath and drew in another. I focused. From faraway, the cottonwoods on the Kirby River smelled sweet, and the damp earth of its banks had an almost metallic fragrance. Although I'd inhaled these scents often over the years, I'd never experienced them as deeply as I did now.

I'm here, I said silently. *Come to me.*

Then I sat back and waited.

I bolted upright at the sound of twigs crackling under footsteps. Sam?

"Josie. Is that you?" It was Lise. "What did you do to your hair?"

I let out a sigh of relief and stood. "You came. It worked." I plucked my velour sweatshirt and released it. "I'm in hiding. Pro tip: black hair isn't great for redheads."

"I was at the café and had the distinct impression you were here and wanted to see me. It was bizarre. I could literally smell you here—the moss, the pine needles, even Rodney's fur." She pulled fingers up his tail, and he nuzzled her hand.

"Magic is weird that way."

"It felt urgent." Lise lifted a white paper sack. "I had Darla pack up the rest of my meal to go. Want part of a grilled cheese?"

"Yes, please."

"They're looking for you in town, you know."

"You came, anyway," I said.

"You're not a murderer. It's your Aunt Beata, isn't it? She's behind it."

I patted the fallen tree trunk next to me, and Lise sat. Rodney jumped up, too, to nose around the food. I hadn't eaten much since breakfast, and that had been skimpy. Even cold, the sandwich was delicious. I picked out a morsel of cheese to feed Rodney.

"People always talk about how good cat fur smells," Lise said, "but it smells even better than that, like narcissus and . . . love." She inhaled. "Emotion furls off you in ribbons. Old leather, saffron. A hint of tarry vetiver. Smells like despair."

"Impressive. I don't even know what vetiver smells like," I said.

Rodney crawled into my lap and purred. He must have been in heaven with two witches so near. He twisted so I could pet his belly, and the star-shaped birthmark where his fur was thin—a twin birthmark to mine—showed.

"Do you feel compelled to use your ability for anything?" I asked.

Lise finished her half of the sandwich and wiped

her fingers. "I don't know. I can't even master muting the scent. It can be too much, and then all of the sudden it fades."

She would figure it out. Eventually. "You hit it on 'despair.' Beata wants me in prison, and she's made a plan to make sure it happens."

"Why didn't she leave town once you freed her magic?"

"She wants to know I can't bind it again. Rodney, leave that alone." He'd been trying to stick his head in the takeaway sack. He looked up at me with a *who, me?* glance. "If I'm in prison, I can't interfere with her. She's plotting to make sure I'm not only arrested for Tyrone's death, but convicted, too."

"How's she going to do that?"

I explained about Byron and the key to Tyrone's room at the Wallingford Guest House. "The key is proof that Byron killed Tyrone. They were on the run from the police. They killed a man in Baltimore. Tyrone may have considered turning himself in, and Byron couldn't have that, so he killed him. Byron overlooked the key. If he remembers and gets rid of it, there goes my proof that he's the murderer and I'm innocent."

"And if Beata gets it. . . ."

My waft of despair had to be pretty strong by now. "Right. The sheriff is getting a search warrant. I need to get that key before Beata plants it in my apartment for him to find." I didn't feel the need to burden Lise with my personal difficulties with Sam at the moment.

"You want my help," Lise said.

"I need it. I'm too new a witch to handle Beata on my own."

She tilted her head. "You're a new witch? Then what good am I?"

"Between us, we command more magic than either of us alone. We'll need to rely more on instinct than experience." That and Grandma's grimoire. "Besides, Beata will come to the library to hide the key, and the library is full of books. I can use their energy as fuel." Simply thinking of the trove of magic, my body warmed.

"Your source," Lise said.

"Exactly." I swiveled to face her. "Will you help me?"

Rodney, the traitor, had now crawled into her lap and purred like an outboard motor. "I don't know how I can. What am I supposed to do, smell her coming?"

I told her the truth. "I don't know what you can do, either. All I know is that if Beata's magic goes unchecked, my going to prison will be the least of it. She could do a lot of damage, ruin a lot of lives."

I felt as if my grandmother spoke through me. Was she here with us? For a moment, I caught an image of her bending to crush pine needles between her fingers. But, no, I'd imagined it. The woods were still but for birds flitting between trees.

"It's a risk for you, too. I don't know how Beata will react. I don't know what she can do. Are you game?" I tried to ask this nonchalantly, but it was my life we would be fighting for. My life most immediately, that was. Perhaps we would save others in the future.

"I want to say no," replied Lise, "but I can't. This is my destiny, somehow. Is that bizarre?"

"As you're finding out, it's not strange at all."

Destiny was a big subject, one I'd grappled with often from my chair by the fire, when fate didn't breathe down my neck as it did now. For me, choice was moot. Justice motivated me. In this case, justice applied not just to Byron, but to Beata. Lise would have to come to her own conclusion.

The seconds stretched to minutes, and Rodney, eyes closed, continued to purr loudly.

"Okay," Lise said finally. "What do you need me to do?"

Chapter Thirty-five

At last, day teetered on the edge of night. I rose and dusted the bark and pine needles from my rear end and gave thanks for the tracksuit's warmth. Lise had left hours ago. I'd kept alert for signs of the sheriff's office, but no one had come here for me yet.

"Come on, Rodney. We're going home."

But not home the usual way. I'd given my key to Lise, and besides, someone from the sheriff's office would undoubtedly be watching for me to return. My lame costume as Ian's mother Escalade—I still groaned at the name—would only get me so far, and might even be public information by now. Luckily, I knew a way into the library that didn't involve a key.

I kept to the trees along the path that led from the woods, along the bluff above the river, to the library. Where the woods thinned near the clearing around the library, I stopped behind an old oak and surveyed the grounds.

The library was completely still, dark. It was closed by now, of course, and Roz had turned off the lights and drawn the curtains. I faced the far side of the old mansion—the side away from the drive to the highway— and only the odd day hiker or Lyndon doing garden duties would see me. At this time of the day, neither was likely.

Rodney at my heels, I ran across the open space and crouched at the library's outer wall, directly outside the former parlor, below the bay windows of what was now Literature. My plan was to shimmy down the saw-dust chute that had once fed the mansion's ancient boiler in the basement. Now, of course, an efficient gas furnace heated the building.

I edged to the hinged steel door in the foundation and pried my fingers under its heavy rim.

"What are you doing?"

I wheeled around to see Buffy and Thor behind me. "What are *you* doing? You're supposed to be home after dark," I said, following the old advice that the best defense is a good offense. I kept my voice low.

"You're a fumigator," Thor said.

"Fugitive," I corrected.

"We're here to look for you," Buffy said. Her sequined tulle skirt was a dusty pink in the twilight. "You're worth big bucks." She squinted. "Why is your hair that color?"

"Someone paid you to find me?"

"They will," Thor said with confidence. "Perhaps Sheriff Sam would be interested in this information?"

A wily smile spread over Buffy's face. "Unless you pay first."

Good grief. These kids made Vito Corleone look like Florence Nightingale. "I don't have my purse with me."

"We'll take an IOU. Here." Buffy proffered a pen and a small notebook with a unicorn on it and the words DREAMS ARE FOREVER.

Shysters. "Is twenty bucks enough?"

"Fifty," Thor said.

"Thirty," I countered.

"Thirty-five, and our silence is only good until tomorrow morning," Buffy said. "After that, we require a supplement."

I snatched the notebook and scrawled out an IOU.

Thor took it, his lips moving as he read. "Who's Escalade Penclosa?"

"Never mind. You got what you wanted, so scram. Grandma Patty is sure to be looking for you. Remember, lips sealed or you don't get a penny, okay?"

Buffy stared at me, her lower lip protruding just barely. She narrowed her eyes, then shifted her gaze to her brother. "Thor, conference."

Thor, who was admiring the IOU for the princely sum, said, "What?"

"We need to talk." Then, to me, "Just a moment, Josie."

Uh-oh. I glanced around. Should I make a run for it? Retreat to the woods?

Just as I pulled myself to standing, Buffy and Thor returned.

"We made a decision," Buffy said. "We're not turning you in, and we're doing it for free."

"For ten dollars only," Thor said.

"No, Thor. We agreed. For free." She rested her hands

on her tutu-adorned hips. "You've been very good to us, and as a gesture of good will, we are providing this service free of charge. Perhaps you'll favor us with your business in the future."

I couldn't nod fast enough. "Definitely."

"Unless the sheriff asks us. Then we need to tell the truth, or Grandma will be mad," Thor added.

Buffy wiped her palms together as if signaling a job well done. "Thor?"

"Good evening, milady," he said. Classic comic books again. "Time to get home for dinner." He grabbed Buffy's hand, and the two kids disappeared around the corner.

I leaned, limp, against the library's side. Close call. I gave myself the luxury of a few seconds of rest before returning to the sawdust chute.

The chute's lid gave with a loud creak and burst of diesel-tinted air as it opened. I froze, but no sirens sounded, and no one came running.

"Are you ready, kitten?" I flipped to my belly and, feet first, slid down the cold, grimy chute. Ancient sawdust tickled my throat. Again, I was grateful for the thickness of the tracksuit's velour. I landed on the basement floor and, coughing, looked up the chute. "You coming?"

Rodney's citrine eyes glowed back. He scampered down like Baryshnikov in a catsuit.

The dust-smeared basement windows gave little light, and I didn't dare flip the light switch. I felt my way to the door to the basement's main hall and inched toward the service stairwell. From there, it was an easy climb to the atrium.

My bones practically melted with the comfort of

thousands of books welcoming me with songs, murmured *hello*s, and a whirlwind of magical energy. Despite my streaky black hair and dirt-encrusted tracksuit, I felt rejuvenated.

I crept up to the tower room to wait.

I let the cooling night air blow over me through the openings of the tower. When would Beata arrive? I was sure she would. And what about Lise? I was tempted to lean forward for a view down the drive, but I didn't dare. My face would show pale against the tower's darkness, and I'd heard an SUV idling at the entrance driveway. A sheriff's deputy.

I'd told Lise to arrive on foot by the forest path, just after dark, and to use my key to enter through the conservatory.

Which didn't mean she'd show up at all. Maybe she'd had second thoughts. She'd watched as I broke the spell binding Beata's magic. She knew what Beata was capable of. Perhaps she'd returned to Astoria. If she had, I couldn't blame her.

Sound funneled up from the atrium. Someone was downstairs. I heard a door slowly open, then steps in the stairwell. I held my breath and half-rose from my chair.

"Josie?"

Lise. I stood and stepped into the hall. She'd come.

The books sensed a new source of magic, and their humming intensified until the library's air vibrated like a beehive. Underlying the buzz sounded a baritone thread of warning: *Don't, careful, no, go.*

Together, we walked down the hall toward my apartment. Lise's penlight made a spot of white-yellow on the fir floorboards.

"I wasn't sure you'd come," I whispered.

"I had to. I admit, though, I'm scared." Lise glanced over the banister, into the library's shadowy depths. "You live up here?"

"The old servants' quarters were made into an apartment when Marilyn Wilfred converted her family home into the library."

"Who's Marilyn Wilfred?"

"Remember the portrait above the entrance to the foyer? The woman in the flapper gown? I showed her to you."

"The one with the black cat at her feet," Lise said. "Yes. She's mesmerizing."

I knew the feeling. I'd always wondered if there was something magical about her, but I never knew for certain. "That's Marilyn Wilfred."

We went into my apartment. A faint glow showed through Sam's kitchen curtains across the garden.

"Stay back," I told Lise, "and you'd better turn off your flashlight." I led her to my bedroom, where a breeze through the window ruffled the partially closed curtains. "If we sit here, on the floor, we won't be seen."

"Next to the bed?" She pointed to the rag rug.

I nodded, although Lise couldn't see me. I'd loved living in this apartment with its Victorian furniture and cozy fireplace. As before, I hoped these would not be my last few hours here.

"I'll light a candle," I said. "We'll need it."

I took the brass candlestick from my bedside table and set it on the floor. Candle lit, I slid the green trunk with my grandmother's magic lessons from under the bed. Rodney was already purring. Would the trunk open with another person near? It wouldn't open for my mother, even though she was also a witch.

I glanced at Lise. The candle cast a pink-orange light on her freckles. I hoped it wasn't a mistake to involve her. "Are you sure you want to go through with this? I don't know what Beata will do to protect her power."

"I have the feeling she'd do just about anything." Lise's gaze wandered to the room's dark edges as if imagining the possibilities. "You can't do this without me. This is where I need to be."

Whatever Lise's magical drive was, it was moral—that much I now knew. I felt a bond to her, as if I'd known her for years. A sisterly feeling. Was it because we both had magic in our veins, or was it something more? "Thank you. I hope I can repay you someday."

"By telling me about my gift, you already have." She nodded toward the trunk. "We'd better get busy. We don't know when she'll turn up."

I rested a hand on the trunk's latch, and it sprang open without any effort on my part. Whatever was about to happen was fated.

The trunk's letters glowed in a blinding blend of red, green, and golden light as if they were living. But it wasn't the letters that caught my eye, it was the grimoire. On its own, the grimoire rose to the top of the letters.

"What is this?" Lise's voice was breathy with wonder.

It took me a moment to be able to speak. "My grandmother's grimoire. She kept her spells in it. Among other things."

"It's as if it's alive."

Lise and I both jumped back as Rodney dropped into the trunk and rolled on the grimoire, purring more loudly than I'd ever heard him.

More strangely, the library's books were singing. Their voices wove together in an eerie music that was half symphony, half chant. They often spoke to me and sometimes sang—especially the books in Arts—but never had they sounded like this.

"Do you hear that, too?" I asked Lise.

"Hear what?"

"Never mind." I slipped the grimoire from under Rodney. It was nearly too hot to touch, yet my hands closed on it like a magnet drew iron. Rodney leapt from the trunk, and I shut it, setting the grimoire on top. It flew open to a page I'd never seen.

"It opened by itself," Lise said, catching her breath.

"It's the spell we need. The spell to bind Beata's magic again."

My fingers trembled. The spell looked to be simply words, no objects needed. That didn't mean the spell would be easy—on the contrary, it would require every atom of magic we could draw. Maybe more than we had. And it would have to be focused with laser-like intensity.

Then the words on the page vanished.

"What happened?" Lise said. "Weird. I smell herbs—rosemary, lavender, and something else. Mugwort."

She looked at me with surprise. "I've never even heard of mugwort."

My grandmother. *You will know what to do* wrote itself on the page, then vanished.

"This is the freakiest thing that's ever happened to me," Lise said.

"That makes two of us, and I'm supposed to be used to it by now."

"What do we do when Beata gets here?" Lise said.

The books' singing was louder, dizzying. My heart beat faster. "I don't know."

"We need some kind of plan." Lise's voice had risen in pitch.

Downstairs, the kitchen door creaked open.

Chapter Thirty-six

"It's her," I said. Rodney slunk to his belly and growled quietly.

Lise was now calm. Somehow, with Beata's arrival, she'd found her strength. "Let's go downstairs."

A cracking sound rent the silence and snapped at the fibers of my muscles. All at once, the books silenced. "She put a spell over the library," I whispered. "Probably to shield it. Make other people look away while she does her business."

"Does she know we're here?" Lise asked.

I listened. Nothing. "I don't know."

Lise's expression didn't change, but she tipped her nose into the air. She looked a lot more sedate than I felt. "Never mind. She knows. Tuberose and sulfur. Come on."

You will know what to do, the grimoire had said. How I hoped it was right.

Beata was in the library's kitchen. I sensed it. Yet when Lise and I came side by side into the atrium, the lamp on the central table was on, and standing near it was Sam, eyes closed. The expression about your heart leaping into your throat? My heart rocketed so fast, it nearly choked me.

Lise's hand dropped to squeeze my fingers. "It's Beata," she whispered.

Then Sam melted into my Aunt Beata. This was young Beata, the beautiful Beata who had seduced my grandfather. Her hair might have been spun from late summer honey, and her smile would have done credit to Botticelli. "Josie. And Lise. I'm so glad to see you."

Beata's glamour was powerful, and I felt my defenses melt. This was the glamour she'd used to uproot her community and destroy my family, the glamour she'd undoubtedly employed to get Tyrone's guest house key from Byron. She would not fool me twice.

Focus. The books began to hum again and feed me their energy, first a trickle, then a stream. Beata's mask dropped. She aged before our eyes, her hair graying, her skin thinning and folding into gentle wrinkles.

Her voice remained powerful. "You cannot stop me. You're nothing but foundlings. My magic—thanks to you"—a lurid smile cracked her face—"will crush yours. Save yourself and give up."

I let the books' magic reverberate within me. "No."

"My plan was to leave the final piece of evidence that would seal your fate. You'd be in prison." A halo grew around Beata. I trembled. "You knew that. You wouldn't be mine if you were that smart."

Mine? What did she mean? Or did she look at Lise? This was Beata's glamour, I reminded myself. Her power. She wanted to confuse us, knock us off balance.

Beata continued. "I will still do that. But since you're here, I'll seal everything up tight. You've saved me a lot of trouble. I'll bind your magic before I make sure you're locked away."

Lise looked at me in panic. Bind my magic? She could do it. In fact, it was possible that Beata was the only witch who could do it, and that was all thanks to me and my tragic misstep in the woods. Yes, Beata was powerful, but I was here, in the library, surrounded by the source of my magic. I had my books.

My birthmark burned on my shoulder as if pierced with hot pins. I raised my hands, and a surge of energy powerful enough to rival lightning, energy fed by centuries of literature, illuminated my body. I was shielded. Beata threw her hands toward me, and fire bounced off the dome. My ears screamed with the text of war novels—firing cannons, shrieking soldiers, arrows tipped with fire. The books possessed me.

At my feet, Rodney had become something fierce. His tail whipped, and ears flattened to his skull.

Beata's eyes narrowed. She turned her hands to the rooms around us, spinning slowly, pointing her fingers first at eye level, then at the floors above. Windows rattled as if a tornado had taken hold of the library, although I knew Wilfred slept peacefully outside us. Lights crackled on and off. Whether this was Beata's magic or mine, I didn't know.

Then fire ripped along the old house's floors, following the trail of Beata's fingers.

No! She was destroying the library—and the books. She was killing the source of my magic.

The books screamed as flames enveloped their shelves. Their pain raked through me.

I half expected Beata to be standing, mouth wide in an evil laugh, but she regarded me calmly. My gaze dropped to Lise, slumped lifeless on the floor.

Rodney yowled, and every hair on my body prickled like needles.

A book glowing green dropped from the sky and hovered in front of Beata. The grimoire!

As I watched, fire raging around me, the book lost shape and remade itself as the beating heart of the ghost of my grandmother. She floated two feet above the floor, her hair waving free, a tranquil smile on her face. Grandma's lips moved as if she spoke, but I heard nothing but the screaming of the books.

I tore my gaze from her. I had to stop the fire. I thrust my hands up again to hurl every micron of energy I could muster against the magic that fueled the flames. My magic hit the edge of my shield and swirled back at me. Beata had sealed it.

Anger and fear suffused me. I was a helpless spectator to my own destruction.

Beata's face was contorted with anger, but the specter of my grandmother, with her grimoire beating in her chest, regarded her serenely. Both women were powerful witches, but family dynamics persevered. Beata was once again the wheedling teenager, and my grandmother the steady older sister. I couldn't hear their conversation. Panic rising, I could only watch their body language and imagine the long-ago drama they rehashed.

Meanwhile, all around me, the library burned. My anger had become a gut-deep sorrow now. What had I done? Why had I been so foolish? Everything—telling Sam I was a witch, freeing Beata's magic, leading Lise into this trap—were fodder for a cannon now loaded with powder and pointed at me. All that had been left was for Beata to light the fuse. And she had.

Then I felt a zap course through me. I looked down. Lise, barely conscious, rested her hands on the dome, meant to protect, that now trapped me. Her fingers, blanched and trembling, moved against the magical wall. At first slowly, then quickly, the spell vaporized, and my magic thrust back into me like jolts from a defibrillator. I widened my stance, raised my arms, and drew in every letter of every book not yet consumed by flames and liquidated it into magic. I'd done this once before—just after I'd come into my magic—but then it had been a frightening accident. My magic had grown since then.

"Fire," I shouted. "Cease!"

Time wound backwards like a movie shown in reverse. Flames shrank and disappeared, rendering books once again whole. Smoke furled in upon itself, and burnt shelves became embers, then merely blackened, then whole again, leaving nothing but a faint smell of smoke, almost like incense. The force of the magic drained me, and I blacked out for a moment.

When I came to, the atrium was dead silent. Nothing was burnt but my grandmother's grimoire, which lay cold and charred on the dark floor. My grandmother was gone. Lise, exhausted, leaned against the wall, her eyes half-closed, one hand resting on Rodney's back.

Where was Beata? I had to get to her. I had to bind her magic.

"Over here." Beata stood at the entrance to the atrium. She was her young self again, irresistible. Her glamour enveloped her like a heady perfume. "You'll never find the key. However, Sam will." She glanced at the grimoire, then at me. She smiled. "You'll soon discover another surprise, as well."

I opened my mouth to speak, but invisible ties gagged me. I couldn't move, either.

"Leaving family is such a trial. Goodbye."

By the time I could summon my magic to free myself, she'd be gone. I'd never find her; she would make sure of that.

She waved and placed a hand on the brass doorknob. At the same time, a long, low creaking sounded above us, and the portrait of Marilyn Wilfred tumbled from its perch of a hundred years. It landed smack on Beata, knocking her out cold.

I swear Marilyn was smiling.

Chapter Thirty-seven

I was exhausted. Utterly, completely, to-the-bone exhausted.

Once the portrait had knocked out Beata, the enchantment holding me hostage had broken. I'd been able to easily bind Beata's magic. Not only did I remove her supercharge of power, I contained all of her magic, leaving behind only a thin residue, no more than anyone had. When she regained consciousness, she was merely a woman in late middle age with traces of her former beauty in her pale eyes and sharp cheekbones, but none of her former glamour. I reached down and peeled her blouse from her shoulder as she looked up, fear in her eyes. The birthmark was gone.

She walked away. I knew I would never see her again.

When the door closed, I turned to Lise, slumped against the wall. I pressed fingers to her neck. Her heart still beat. "Lise? Lise, wake up."

Her eyes fluttered open, then closed again.

I knelt next to her. "Lise. Wake up. It's okay now."

She struggled to sitting and rubbed her eyes. "What happened?"

I explained how Beata had put a spell on her, but that she'd saved me by dissolving the dome Beata had sealed over me.

"I did that?" she said.

Lise was just coming into her magic. It would take time for it to settle in, and what form it might take, I didn't know.

"I am so tired." She pulled herself to standing. She'd tipped up her face and inhaled. "The sulfur is gone. It smells good in here again, like old books and calm."

"I'm wiped out, too," I'd said. "Can you make it back to the retreat center alone?"

Now Lise was back at the retreat center for what I guessed would be the deepest sleep she'd ever experienced. As for me, I was so tired that I questioned whether I had even the energy to mount the stairs to my apartment.

Besides that, one tiny thought niggled at me. Beata had said, "You'll soon discover another surprise." What could it be? I didn't have the strength to worry about it. Besides, now that her magic was gone, Beata wouldn't be able to try any further assaults.

I sank to the floor, next to Marilyn's fallen portrait. I'd get up soon and go to bed. I simply needed a moment to catch my breath.

The sound of metal on metal broke the silence. Rodney growled low in his throat. Someone was messing with the lock on the kitchen door. Or was it the window in Old Man Thurston's office on the opposite side of the library? Sounds seemed to come from both directions.

Before I could pull myself to standing, Byron Marshall strode into the atrium, a long zip tie dangling from his belt. I couldn't breathe. It was if the zip tie were already tightened around my chest, squeezing the air from my lungs.

He seemed surprised to see me on the floor, but it only stopped him a second. He smiled and crossed the atrium. "Well, well, Josie the librarian." His expression turned deadly serious. "Give me the key."

The key. That was one detail I hadn't yet settled. "I don't have it."

He grabbed my collar and yanked me to my feet. "Stop playing around. I saw you take the key."

Then I understood. This was the "surprise." When Beata's magic had vanished, so, too, did the spell of glamour she'd cast on Byron. Now he remembered seeing Tyrone's room key taken from his van. The thing was, Beata had veiled herself as me. He thought it was me who'd taken the key.

There was no way I could talk myself out of this one.

"If you won't give me the key, I'll have to find it myself," Byron said. His breath was sour with beer.

Even if I had a scintilla of energy left, I wouldn't be able to wriggle from his grasp. I closed my eyes and willed the books to lend me their strength. They, too, were depleted. I'd wrung them, and myself, dry.

"I don't know what you're talking about," I said.

"Liar."

He whipped the zip tie from his belt. This was it, then. I'd vanquished a powerful witch only to be killed by a sociopathic street gangster. Rodney hissed and struck at Byron's ankles, but he kicked him away.

Byron looped the zip tie around my neck and fed the end through its latch.

"Don't do this," I whispered. Rodney yowled.

All at once, Byron's head jerked, and he released me.

I stumbled back to see Wanda, dressed all in black, delivering a sharp blow to Byron's skull. Byron quickly recovered his balance and turned toward her, one arm extended to grab her neck. If I'd thought Wanda's flamenco dancing was graceful, it was nothing compared to her kickboxing skills. She shouted, "Ay-*ya*!" and kicked high, spun, then delivered a series of one-two punches that made David Carradine in *Kung Fu* look like an amateur.

Byron was as shocked as I was. Eyes wide, he stumbled sideways. Almost before I entirely understood what was happening, he lay unconscious on the floor, handcuffed with his own zip tie. I stared first at him, then at Wanda, her face blackened, a dark stocking cap pulled over her gray hair. Only her eyeballs showed white. Behind her lay a garbage sack.

"Wanda . . . ?"

She breathed heavily for a moment, then ripped off her cap. "I'm losing my mind."

"What are you doing here?"

She burst into loud, body-wracking sobs. "I'm having a nervous breakdown."

I led her to a chair, and she sat, no resistance. Rodney surprised me by jumping into her lap, and Wanda surprised me even more by, still sobbing, petting him.

"I . . . I'm a bad person," she said. She paused, petting Rodney long enough to pull off a black glove and blow her nose into it.

"You're a good person," I said. "You saved my life." I needed to call the sheriff's office. Byron wouldn't stay unconscious for long.

"No, I'm not. I came here to steal books from the kids' section." She waved toward the garbage sack.

"Books about cats," I said.

At that, Rodney jumped from her lap and trotted purposefully from the room.

Wanda nodded in bewilderment. "Yes. And throw them in the river." Her sobbing quieted, but the tears still flowed. "I've completely gone 'round the bend. Who have I become?"

Remembering Duke's story about her broken engagement, I said, "You've been under a lot of stress."

"That's no excuse. I jimmied Old Man Thurston's office window and crawled in. Then I saw you and that man. . . ."

I retrieved a box of tissues from Circulation and handed it to her.

"Somehow," she said, "seeing him threatening you, it all came to me at once, and I thought, *what am I doing?* I'm actually breaking into a library to . . . to steal children's books." She looked at me with tear-filled eyes. "Then, boom! I was angry. Like, really angry. I had some"—she glanced at me—"disappointments lately, and I hadn't felt a whit of anger. Just now it all came roaring in." Her hands flopped to her sides. "Wow." She sniffed and, ignoring the box of tissues, honked into her glove again.

She'd sure chosen the right way to express that anger. "Excuse me a moment. Don't go anywhere."

As I climbed the service stairs to call 911, I heard my phone chiming, over and over. I fetched it from the side table and watched text after text flood its screen. Emotion thickened in my throat as the messages appeared. I only caught glimpses of them—*see you, love you, when, why.* The number on my voicemail box ticked up, too. All from Sam. Realization dawned. To make my life worse and so build my need for her, Aunt Beata had been blocking Sam's communication. Now that she was banished, the spell had snapped. All those texts and calls had been released.

I ran downstairs, phone in hand, and nearly collided with Sam, also holding his phone. "Sam."

"Josie," he said.

I fell into his arms. This was home. The salty smell of his skin, his warm embrace. Complete, utter happiness. I yanked myself away. "Let's talk. But first, I need you to arrest a murderer."

I grabbed his hand—that wonderful strong hand—and pulled him into the atrium, where Byron was coming to, his wrists still tightly bound behind him. Wanda stood guard over him, looking like a cross between Johnny Cash and a ninja.

Rodney nosed between us and dropped something on Byron's chest.

It was Tyrone's room key.

Chapter Thirty-eight

A few hours later, in my apartment, Sam cradled my head on his chest. "I thought you didn't want me, that I hadn't responded right when you told me about your. . . ." he said.

"That I'm a witch," I finished.

After Sam had seen Byron Marshall and questioned him briefly, he'd arrested him and called backup to take him to jail. Between the key, Wanda's testimony, and Byron's status as a fugitive, it was a good bet Byron would never see the outside of a correctional institution again. When the sheriff's deputies left, Sam had followed me upstairs.

"I needed time to let your news about being a witch sink in," he told me. "That's all. I texted you the next morning to see if we could talk, but you never responded."

"I know," I'd said dreamily.

"This witch thing," he said, "it's not such a crazy

idea to me as you might think. I tried to tell you, but you didn't reply to my texts or calls. Then I had to leave town for work. Maybe, I thought, the time apart would give you the chance to think things through. I'd hoped you'd want to talk with me when I returned. Then I saw you coming out of the tavern with Tyrone Beaudrie."

I ran a hand over Sam's arm. "Nothing was going on there. Tyrone was no you."

Sam kissed the top of my head. "I know that now. I thought I'd done wrong by not telling you right away, on the spot, that I had no problem with your magic, that I was more familiar with witches than you knew."

I lifted my head. "What do you mean?"

"Aunt Marilyn. There was always something special, a little *off*, about her. People in town loved her, but in her earlier years, they feared her. Maybe you've heard stories?"

I had. I'd seen photos, too, of Marilyn with her dark gaze, standing apart from others.

"Then I stumbled upon her organizing the bookshelves just by looking at them."

"You were there?"

"Remember, I had a key to the library, even as a kid. I let myself in one evening to get the next Hardy Boys mystery. Aunt Marilyn must not have heard me. I was in the atrium, and I saw her gesture toward the rolling shelf, the one you use to put books away—"

I nodded. I knew that shelf well.

"—and the books rose into the air and sailed off to their homes throughout the library, all by themselves. I couldn't believe it. When I asked her about it, she just smiled and said I had an overactive imagination. After that night, I noticed other things, too."

"Like what?"

"For one, she always seemed to know the book I wanted even before I told her. Sometimes I saw her talking when no one was there. After a while I figured out she was talking to books. Also, like you, she had a black cat who followed her around."

I could picture them together—Marilyn, the witch, and her nephew with the quiet way and piercing observations, the boy who smiled when he was angry and frowned when upset. They were both oddballs and both remarkable people.

I rested my head again on his chest. "Tell me one more time how you tried to get in touch with me."

Sam said he'd left me notes and flowers, but I'd never received them. Again, Beata's work. I told him about her plan to separate us and her plot to have me release her magic.

"The crows," he said. "There were so many crows, even at night. I'd wondered about that."

It was so nice to talk freely with someone else about witchcraft, and I hoped he'd be my confidant for decades to come. I didn't tell Sam about Lise—that was her secret to reveal or not, as she chose. For a solid hour, we discussed our pasts, our future, and magic.

"I always wondered about Aunt Marilyn," he said again, "then when you showed me your magic. . . ."

I didn't hear the rest. I'd fallen asleep.

* * *

"I call the library trustees' meeting to order," Ruth Littlewood said from the podium, set up once again, in the library's atrium.

The excitement from two days earlier had been nearly erased. Marilyn's portrait hung above the entry once again, with only a chip in its gilded frame as witness to its job subduing Beata. Wanda's mental collapse when she broke into the library was on the mend, too. Duke said she was seeing a counselor, and she was looking into work as a kickboxing instructor. I hadn't heard a peep from her about cat books.

After a few nights of rest, my magic was back at its former levels. Even better, a few hours of Candace's ministrations at the Beauty Palace had returned my hair to its natural red color.

Tonight, the atrium again teemed with Wilfredians, some eager to learn what would happen with the children's books, and others there simply for the drama. Mother Tohler chatted with Ian and Lalena, who still wore the engagement ring.

"You'll want children," she said. "Lots of them."

"Silence, everyone," Ruth said, and we quieted. As before, she turned over the podium to Wanda.

"Thank you for coming," Wanda said. Again she wore a suit, but there was something more open about her tonight. She smiled, and it wasn't at all forced. "Our last meeting was very instructive. In the intervening days, I've come to a realization."

"That cats are important members of our society," Mona said.

"Not that," Wanda replied.

Despite her words, I'd noticed a softening of Wanda's

attitude toward Rodney and vice versa. Rodney was happy to lounge in the same room with her, and I'd even caught Wanda once absently petting him while thumbing through books in the self-help section. If Mona played her cards right, she might even eventually find a home for one of her foster charges.

"No, my realization isn't about cats, but about the role of a library. A library is a place where we can all come to learn, be entertained, and gain inspiration. It's a place where we can challenge ourselves to understand other views." Wanda placed her hands flat on the podium and regarded them a moment. "My mistake was to try to force my beliefs on others. Instead, I should have moved to share my beliefs with you, to give you the opportunity to consider something new."

From her seat behind Wanda, Ruth clapped. "Brava!"

"To that end, I propose the library host a monthly discussion forum where people can present their views and answer questions. We can debate not just cats and birds, but all sorts of issues."

This was perfect. I stood. "Thank you, Wanda. What an excellent idea. If people sign up ahead of time, and we might even be able to find experts to come and speak. We could offer modest honorariums."

People in the crowd nodded here and there. "Seems reasonable to me," Duke said.

"I'd go for that," Mrs. Tohler added. "I've already been making notes."

"In the meantime. . . ." Wanda didn't seem to be able to finish.

"Yes?" I said.

"In the meantime, the cat books remain," she said quickly, and sat down.

When the meeting broke up, a new mood had descended on the library. I stood on the library's porch to wave goodbye to Wilfredians walking down the hill toward home.

Parting the crowds, Lise's Kia slowly approached. I crossed the gravel drive to meet her. We'd spent hours together over the past few days, walking in the woods and talking about magic. I felt a kinship with her, and I couldn't help but remember Beata's words. Were we cousins—or even sisters? I'd questioned my mother, but her mind was curiously blank. I'd follow up.

Lise stepped from her car and hugged me. The faint scent of dark summer flowers clung to her, likely another vintage perfume she'd rescued from a thrift shop or estate sale. "I couldn't leave Wilfred without saying goodbye."

"It's been great to get to know you," I said.

That was an understatement. In the past week, everything had changed, and Lise had been a part of it. I looked at her, so familiar yet so different, like catching a glimpse in a mirror of a more stylish yet more bohemian version of myself.

"We'll see each other again," Lise said. "Astoria isn't far."

"We'll definitely see each other again," I said. "I guarantee it."

Visit our website at
KensingtonBooks.com
to sign up for our newsletters, read
more from your favorite authors, see
books by series, view reading group
guides, and more!

BOOK · CLUB
BETWEEN THE CHAPTERS

Become a Part of Our
Between the Chapters Book Club
Community and Join the Conversation

Betweenthechapters.net